Bug Out! Part 1

Escape In a Motorhome

Robert G Boren

Chapter 1 - Lock Down and Leave

Jane stared out the upstairs window, a worried look on her face. There was smoke rising into the air, several miles to the east. The sea breeze was blowing it inland.

"It's getting closer," she said to herself.

"What?"

Jane turned around. Frank was out of bed, walking towards her. He looked out the window.

"Oh, remains of last night's festivities, huh?"

Jane looked up at him. He was much taller than she was, and still had a lot of vigor for being in his early 60s. She was in good health too, for her 57 years. One of her friends had joked that they looked like they just walked out of a retirement finance commercial.

"These thugs are getting closer to us," Jane said. "What're we going to do when they're at our doorstep?"

"I've been thinking a lot about that. We're locked into this condo, but we don't have to live here all the time."

"Locked in?"

"Meaning we can't sell out and move without ruining ourselves financially."

"Oh."

"We do have an asset that we can use until things get back to normal, though."

"Are you going to start that stuff about the motorhome again?" asked Jane.

"Yes, as a matter of fact."

"I don't want to full time in the RV."

"Neither do I. Look at it like being a snowbird," he said. "Winter is here, and it would be nice to be away. When winter is over, we come back home to South Bay."

"Is winter going to be over?" She looked at him as he collected his thoughts.

"I still have hope, sweetheart. People are finally starting to get pissed, and eventually they'll start voting the idiots out."

"It's going to be a long road, and the problems are tough," Jane said. "How do you tell a government employee that they have to take less in retirement? That's something they've worked for. They're counting on it."

"You can't," Frank said. "There has to be other ways to solve the problems, until we have more balance between young and old in this state. The problem is that nobody wants to make the tough choices."

"Well, let's not go into politics, or we'll just get into a fight again."

"Agreed."

"So tell me about your idea, Frank, and I'll try to keep an open mind."

"My idea is simple. The coach is already pretty well stocked up from the trip last month. I say we grab the rest of the stuff we need, throw the dog and the cat into the car, and take off for the storage yard. We have to go early in the day, though...lots of places between here and San Bernardino that I wouldn't want to drive through after dark."

"OK, we get to the coach. Then what?"

"Head to Arizona or Nevada, and just hang out. Watch and listen. Be nimble on our feet, move around when we need to, and come back when the government has a handle on things here."

"Aren't you worried about the condo when we're gone?" asked Jane.

"Of course, but if something bad happens, wouldn't you rather have it happen when we aren't around?"

Jane looked down, thinking. She couldn't come up with a good counter to that.

"What about the kids?"

"Sarah's already living far enough away. I think she'll be fine. I've tried to talk Robbie into moving, but he isn't hearing me. Bottom line, we can't force him to move just because it would make us feel more comfortable. That's really up to him."

"Can we afford it? It's going to be hard to boondock much with that residential fridge running down the batteries. RV Parks cost a lot."

"We were going to add solar and the extra batteries anyway. Let's just move that up. We have the park discount memberships, which will help us with the cost some, and remember, we won't be moving around as much. This isn't a vacation. We can take advantage of the longer term rates when we find a place that will make a good long term stop."

"You won't go stir crazy living in the small space?"

"Are you kidding? Who's the one who always wants to stay out longer?"

"I know, I know," Jane said. "I guess that one was stupid…I'm never quite ready to come home either, but I love our sticks and bricks house."

"We aren't giving it up forever. Just for a while."

"Unless somebody comes along and burns it down."

"We have insurance, honey, and like I said, I'd rather not be here if something like that happens. We can replace the house, but if we burn up with it, it's game over."

Jane walked from the window into the kitchen. She turned on the coffee maker, and got a couple of cups down out of the cupboard. Frank followed her in there, and sat down at the kitchen table. They could still see the billow of smoke rising, and now there were helicopters circling. They both stared silently out the window as the coffee machine sputtered.

"Want me to turn on the news, sweetie?" asked Frank.

"Not on my account. We know what happened. I'm sick of hearing about it every day." She came over to the table with a cup of coffee in each hand. "Here you go, honey."

Frank took his cup and had a sip.

"How soon do we need to decide?" asked Jane.

"Sooner the better, as far as I'm concerned. If you want to go slow, we can watch and see what the gangs do over the next week or so. Maybe wait to see what the Governor does. If he calls out the National Guard that might stop the looting."

"You don't look very hopeful."

"A lot of people to the east have left, and the pickings are getting slimmer and slimmer over there. More people stuck around in our area, and they have more money. That means more stuff to cart off. Easy picking, big payoff."

"What about the National Guard?"

Frank smiled. "That's going to lead us to politics again."

Jane sighed. "Go ahead and tell me what you're thinking."

"The governor waited too long. He didn't call them out to protect people in the poor and lower middle class areas, and he's taking a lot of heat for that. Guess what'll happen when he finally calls them out for the upper middle class areas."

"Urrrggggg," she said. "Forget I asked."

"Alright."

"You want to leave tomorrow morning, don't you?"

"Yeah, because it's only going to get harder to get out of here if we wait. We can lock down the house today and be ready to go at sunup."

"Can we really be ready that quickly?"

"I think so. The long pole in the tent will be getting that security system set up."

"You want to do that before we leave?"

"Yes."

"It's not going to stop anybody from coming in here."

"I know, but it will allow us to see what's going on. We'll have access to the cameras via the internet."

"Why does that matter?" asked Jane.

"Well, if we have broken windows or a door hanging open, I can call somebody to go fix it. That should limit the damage."

Jane nodded. She looked out the window, deep in thought. Frank knew to shut up for a few minutes. He got up and got another cup of coffee.

"Alright, I'll do it," said Jane. She got up from the table and walked over to Frank. "Are you really sure we'll be safer?"

"Yes, because we won't be where the gangs are. And if things get bad where we are, we leave and find a new place."

"I'll start putting things that we need into boxes. I think our papers and as many photos as we can carry should go with us."

"Anything really valuable that isn't too big should go into the safety deposit boxes."

"Agreed. I'll take care of that while you get the security system installed."

Frank went downstairs to the garage. He turned on the fluorescent light over the workbench, and looked around. His sports car was sitting next to the far wall, and the Jeep Liberty was sitting closest to the door, next to the work bench. He was glad that he had the Liberty ready to tow. That was the last major project he finished for their RV.

The garage had two doors – a wide rollup garage door and a walk through door on the opposite wall, which led to a tiny side yard. The rollup door was pretty secure. He could unplug the garage door opener on the way out. The walk through door just had the normal dead bolt and door knob. Not secure enough, since the door was not visible from the street. It wasn't far from the end of his work bench. Maybe I can block it with something, he thought to himself. Then he remembered the four by fours that he had against the wall behind his sports car. He climbed back over there. Yes, that would do nicely, he thought. He picked up the first one. It was six foot long and heavy. He carried it carefully around the cars, and over to the door. It was longer than the space he had between the end of the work bench and the door. He leaned one end of the timber up against the back door, and the other end slid back on the floor and hit the bottom frame of the heavy workbench.

"Son of a bitch," he said to himself, smiling and shaking his head. The timber was wedged between the work bench and the door, with the timber sitting against the door about four feet off of the floor. "Nobody is getting past that."

The security system was in a big box sitting on the work bench. He opened it. Inside were four cameras, a DVR unit, and a control box. There was a lot of wire included. It took him a couple of hours to get everything laid out, and the garage camera installed.

Frank heard footsteps coming down the stairs. Jane appeared, with a heavy looking bag under her arm.

"I've got the stuff for the safety deposit box. I'm going to the bank now," she said. Then she glanced over at the back door with the four by four wedged in. "Wow, nobody is coming through there."

Frank just nodded at her and smiled.

Jane fired up the car and backed out, then drove down the driveway. Frank closed the big door and got back to work.

"Well, where should I locate the rest of these cameras?" Frank asked himself. "One pointing down the hall at the front door, one under the eave on the balcony pointing down onto the driveway, and one in the living room." He wished he had more cameras, but the eight camera version cost more than double the $250 that this system cost.

Running the wires for the cameras took the most time. He got it done in just under two hours. He set up the DVR and control box in his office, right next to the cable modem and router. He plugged everything in and turned on the system. Then he went through the steps to get his smart phone and iPad hooked up for remote viewing and management. He was just finishing up when he heard the garage door opening. Jane came walking up the stairs, with a couple bags of groceries.

"There are more bags down there, honey."

"I'm on it," Frank said. He went down the stairs and fetched the remaining bags, taking them to the kitchen.

"Jane, hand me your phone and I'll set you up on the security system."

Jane walked over to her purse and pulled it out. She handed it to Frank.

"Saw the cameras," she said. "Must have been fairly easy to set up."

"I was pleasantly surprised. How did your errands go?"

"They went well. All the stuff that I took to the safety deposit box fit, barely. Then it was off to the store. I picked up enough stuff to keep us going for several weeks."

"Excellent."

"It's weird out there. I had to wait for a bank manager to let me into our safety deposit box, and he asked all kinds of questions. I had to show two forms of ID. And then there was the grocery store. The shelves are getting bare. Looks like a hurricane is coming. There was a big sign up front that said they were closing at 6:00."

"Sounds like everybody is getting ready for martial law."

"I'm glad we're getting out of here," said Jane. "Could you bring up the ice chest? I want to get it packed tonight."

"Will do," Frank said, as he turned to go downstairs.

The rest of the day was consumed with packing. Clothes, medications, electronics, food, and supplies for the cat and the dog. The cat didn't like all of this commotion one bit, and was hiding out all afternoon and into the early evening. The dog was getting excited. Lucy was a little Jack Russell, always bouncing around, but when she saw that camping trip prep was going on, she was just beside herself with excitement.

At about eight pm they were done and tired. Frank flopped down on the recliner sofa and pulled the lever to get his feet up. Jane came over and sat next to him, leaning up against him and putting her hand on his chest.

"I hope we're doing the right thing," she said.

"We are. Trust me."

"Are you bringing the guns?"

"Some of them," Frank said. "The revolver, the Winchester lever gun, and the pump shotgun."

"That's all? No hunting rifles?"

"I think the Winchester and the pump are the only long guns that I can keep out of sight easily, because they're both so short. They give us all the capability we need. No reason to bring too much."

"What if you have to hunt for food?"

"The Winchester will work for that," he said. "You know that if we get stopped and searched on the way to the storage yard, we'll probably lose the guns. I don't want to be giving a two thousand dollar Weatherby to the cops. The high end guns can stay in the gun safe."

"Why would they take them away? They're legal."

“They shouldn’t, but remember what happened during Katrina.”

“Not that again.”

“You asked. Anyway, that means we don’t have to bring as many different kinds of ammo, too.”

“Okay. What time to you want to get up?”

“How about 5:30?”

“I’m good with that. I’ll go set the alarms. Let’s go to bed early.” She got up off the couch, and started towards the bedroom.

“I’m just going to watch some news. I’ll be up in a little while.”

Jane looked out the bedroom window before climbing into bed. There was already a glow of fire to the east. At least it wasn’t any closer than the fire from last night. She laid down and looked up at the ceiling in the dark. Was this the last time she was going to enjoy her nice bed in her condo? She felt unbearably sad. She was just starting to drift off when she heard Frank come in. The bed moved as he carefully climbed in. Jane turned towards him.

“Any news worth talking about?” she asked quietly.

“Not really. The usual talking heads bullshit about martial law and what Washington was going to do. There were some eyewitness accounts of military vehicles coming down from the Bakersfield area, but there wasn't any official comment on that."

Frank brought his hand up and petted Jane's hair, and then moved over and kissed her forehead. They cuddled. Soon they were both fast asleep.

Frank awoke to a loud bang outside. It sounded like it was right down the street. Lucy was barking like crazy. He broke into a cold sweat.

"What was that?" asked Jane, trying to shake off the deep sleep she was in.

"I don't know, but I'm going to find out."

"Don't go outside."

"I'll just go out on the balcony." He left the bedroom, grabbing the shotgun as he went. Lucy was bouncing up and down, barking and growling. Frank opened up the sliding glass door on the balcony and quietly slipped out. He heard breaking glass down the street. Then he saw several people running around in the parking lot of the apartment building two doors down. A woman screamed, and a man's voice yelled 'Shut up'.

Jane poked her head out onto the balcony, the dog in her arms. "What's going on?" she whispered.

"Thugs in the parking lot behind the apartment building over there," Frank whispered back. He pointed. Then something caught his eye. He looked down his driveway, and there were half a dozen dark figures walking past. One of them looked down the driveway, and pointed. He walked down with another person, while the rest of the group continued down the street. Frank waited until they got close, and then cocked the shotgun as loudly as he could. The two stopped and looked up at him.

"Go elsewhere," said Frank in a gruff voice. He could see their faces now, under the glow of his porch light. They were little more than children. They both put their hands up as if to say "alright", and they ran back down the driveway.

"What happened?" whispered Jane.

"It was a couple of kids. I let them see the shotgun, and they ran."

"Thank God," Jane said.

"I'm going to hang out up here for a little while. What time is it?"

"It's 4:30 already."

"Good, it's going to be light pretty soon. Go try to get a little more sleep."

"Not happening," Jane said. "I'm going to start getting things ready."

"Okay."

Frank sat in the cool morning air, listening. He couldn't hear anymore commotion outside. Probably just scouts, he thought to himself. It got light sooner than he expected.

"Frank, could you catch the cat and put him in the carrier?"

"Sure. It's getting too light now for our guests to be around. We can take off any time."

"Good."

Frank went looking for the cat, finding it under the bed. He managed to get him out without too much trouble, and stuffed him into the carrier. The cat started a frequent meow, just like he always did when he was put in there.

"Got him," said Frank as Jane was walking into the bedroom.

"Good. I've got everything lined up by the top of the stairs."

Alright, I'll put Mr. Wonderful's carrier down in the back seat, and then I'll come up and start getting the rest of the stuff carried down."

It took several trips up and down the stairs to get everything. He packed it quickly into the car.

"I'm ready to open the garage door, honey," Frank said. "Why don't you back out the Jeep, then I'll close the garage door and pull the electrical plug."

Jane nodded, and opened the driver's side door. The dog jumped in right away. She got behind the wheel and started the engine as the garage door was coming up. She backed out. When she was clear, Frank closed the garage door, and unplugged the opener when it was all the way down. He double checked the back door, and then went to the stairwell, closed the door, and locked the dead bolt. He climbed the stairs, and then went through each room in the unit, checking the security system cameras, making sure that everything was turned off, and checking all of the windows. When he was satisfied, he went to the front door. The door creaked as he opened it. He turned back to take one more look into the condo, then sighed, and stepped out, closing the door behind him. He locked the deadbolt, and went down the walkway that led to the driveway.

Jane had the car pointed at the street, ready to leave. She rolled down the window.

"Do you want to drive?" she asked.

"You can drive the first stretch, if you'd like," he replied. He went to the passenger side and got in. Lucy jumped on his lap and licked him in the face, her tail wagging. Jane drove away.

The neighborhood on the way to the freeway onramp was littered with broken glass and trash. Police cruisers slowly crept down the streets, the officers looking around cautiously. One of them pulled up next to the Jeep and peered in. Frank looked over at the officer and waved. Satisfied that Frank and Jane weren't trouble makers, the officer waved them on. In a few minutes they were on the freeway, heading east.

“Whew, I thought that cop was going to pull us over and search,” Frank said.

“Me too. We should be alright now, though. I’m surprised how little traffic there is.”

“Nobody wants to be out on the roads," Frank said. "Something is going to break around here. We're getting out just in time, I'm afraid.”

Jane nodded. Then she pointed to westbound lanes.

“Look, military vehicles. A whole bunch of them,” she said.

“Good. Maybe the Governor is going to do the right thing.”

“Hopefully.”

The drive was uneventful after that, and Frank was getting sleepy. He dozed off and slept for a little while. He woke up with a start when he felt them rolling up the freeway off ramp.

"We're here already?"

"Yes," Jane said, sounding concerned.

"What's wrong?"

"Look over there, Frank. More fires. Big ones." She pointed off to the right. Then she got to the top of the ramp and waited for the traffic light to turn green.

"Well, it doesn't look like there are any in the direction of our storage lot," Frank said.

Jane nodded. The light turned green, and she turned left. At the next street, she turned to the right. Their yard was only a couple of blocks down.

"There it is," Frank said. Jane slowed down and made the right turn onto the driveway.

"Shit, look at that," she said.

"Dammit," said Frank. There was a large, ugly homemade trailer blocking the gate, parked across the entire span. It looked like it was made out of an old shipping container.

"What now?"

"Honk the horn," Frank said. "Maybe the owner put that there to protect the place."

Jane honked the horn twice. There was a metallic clank, and a man's torso appeared on the roof of the trailer. The man was holding a gun. He cocked it, and pointed it at the Jeep. Jane and Frank looked at each other, and then back at the angry looking man.

Chapter 2 - Eastbound and Down

"Whoa," Frank said. "Put your hands up on the inside of the windshield."

Jane looked over at Frank, and then did as he asked. The man in the trailer still had the gun on them. Frank rolled down his window and stuck his head out.

"Our motorhome is in there. I have the code for the gate. We need to get in."

"Come out of the car with your hands up," shouted the man.

"Alright, don't shoot. We don't have weapons on us," Frank said, and he nodded at Jane to get out of the car.

"Move away from the car, and stand next to each other over there," said the man, pointing over to the sidewalk that led into the office.

"Call Harry, he knows us," Frank said. "We're legit."

"Been trying to call Harry all morning. No answer. He lives over there." The man pointed off to the south west, where there was a large plume of smoke.

"So what are we going to do?" asked Frank.

"You two need to go home, and come back later," the man said.

“Not happening. We can’t go home. Things are crazy there. That’s why we're here to get the motorhome. We're going east.”

The man cocked his rifle. “I’m not going to ask you again.”

Frank was getting mad now.

“You go ahead and shoot me if you want to, but I’m calling the police right now.”

The man laughed. “They're a little busy right now.”

“Yeah, well I’ll report a man holding a gun on innocent people. I know where the station is. They’ll be here in about three minutes.”

Jane looked up at Frank. She had a terrified look on her face.

“How do you know this guy works for Harry?” she whispered. He looked back at her with his ‘trust me’ look.

The man on the trailer brought his gun up to his shoulder.

“Leave now. I’m not going to tell you again.” He aimed the rifle at Frank.

Just at that moment, an SUV pulled into the driveway behind the Jeep Liberty. A man jumped out.

“Gary, put down the gun,” he shouted.

“OK, boss.” He set down the gun, and climbed off the trailer.

"Harry," Frank said, walking over to him. "Boy are we glad to see you."

The two men shook hands. Harry was about the same age as Frank. They went back a few years.

"Sorry about this, Frank. I hired Gary to keep people from breaking in. The only weak spot in this place is the front gate. The thugs have already hit about half of the RV lots around here."

"You really think this guy should be pointing guns at people?" Jane asked.

"When it's dark, yes. I was late. Didn't figure on that. I'm sorry, Jane."

Gary came walking over, giving Frank an embarrassed look.

"Sorry, man. No offense."

"None taken," Frank said. They shook hands.

"What happened, Harry?" Gary asked. Harry got a grim look on his face, and then looked like he was about to cry, his eyes becoming glassy.

"They hit our street again last night."

"Your place OK?"

"Yeah, Gary, my place is OK. It was the neighbor's house. Remember Kalinda?"

"She was at the BBQ you had a few months ago," Gary said. "Pretty girl. Her dad was a riot. Can't remember his name."

"Luis. His name was Luis," Harry said. He broke down crying. Jane got next to him and touched his shoulder. Frank stood there looking at Harry, not knowing what to say.

"What happened, boss?"

Harry stopped crying and got an angry look on his face.

"Kalinda was walking down the street, coming home from a friend's house. It was only about half a block away. A truck full of gang bangers saw her. They piled out and chased her into her front lawn. Then one of them raped her."

"That's horrible," Jane said. "How old is she?"

"She was only sixteen."

"Was?"

"Yes, Jane, was. Luis saw what was happening and ran out into the front yard with a baseball bat. He brained the guy on top of Kalinda. I think the guy's dead. Then one of the gang bangers shot Kalinda, and then Luis."

"Shit," Gary said. "I'm so sorry."

"Some of us on the street saw what happened, and got our guns out. We killed three of them before they were able to drive away. They'll be back tonight. They always get revenge."

"Is your family still there?" asked Frank.

"No, I sent my wife and daughter to her sister's house in Las Vegas."

"What are you going to do, boss?" asked Gary.

"I'm going to move in here. It's safer than home at this point. My car is full of stuff."

"Why don't you leave?" asked Jane. "Go be with your wife and daughter."

"I can't lose this place, Jane," he said. "It's all I've got."

"Shall I let these folks in?" asked Gary.

"Of course, of course. Bring the fork lift around, and we'll roll the trailer out of the way."

Gary nodded, and went over to the keypad next to the gate. He entered the code, and the gate rolled open.

"Where are you guys headed?" asked Harry.

"East," Frank replied. Jane nodded in agreement.

"Good that you guys are leaving now. I was listening to the radio on the way over here. The Governor finally called out the National

Guard. I think they'll be locking down the state in the next forty-eight hours."

"Locking down the state?" asked Jane. She had a worried look on her face.

"To round up the bad guys before they start flooding out," Harry said. "You may run into a checkpoint even today."

"Shoot, we need to get our butts out of here," Frank said.

"You got gas in your rig?"

"Yep, topped her off after our trip last month."

"Good, smart move," Harry said. He saw the forklift rolling over. The pallet blades each had trailer balls on the end. Gary maneuvered over to the trailer hitch and lifted the blades. The trailer lurched upwards in the front. Then he started slowly pushing the trailer out of the way.

"You folks can go on in and get your rig ready. I'll watch for you, and open the gate when you're ready."

"Thanks, Harry. Let's go, honey."

They climbed back into the Jeep and drove back to their space. Lucy jumped up on Jane's lap and licked her in the face. Frank was looking at the high wall in the back of the lot, and noticed some razor wire hanging down. He parked the jeep next to their rig, and then trotted back over to the gate as Jane got out with the dog.

"Harry, take a look back here. Somebody was trying to get in. The razor wire has been cut in one spot, and it's dangling."

"Oh, shit," Harry said. "Gary, get the gate shut while I go in the back and check this out."

Jane unlocked the door of the coach, and got in. She raised the blinds in the front to let some more light in, as Lucy scampered up the steps. Her tail was wagging like crazy as she sniffed her favorite spots in the coach.

Frank and Harry stood in front of the back fence, looking up. Harry laughed.

"Must have been a nasty surprise seeing that big drop there. It will be tough to find a ladder tall enough for that."

"They could get in with some rope," Frank said. Gary was walking up.

"Hey, boss, I have an idea. Why don't I go get Hank and Crank? I'll stay here for a while with you, and they can help us keep an eye on things at night."

"Hank and Crank?" Frank asked.

"Those are Gary's two Rottweilers."

"Really, boss, I'd be glad to do it. You don't have to pay me for extra hours or anything."

"Alright, but I'll cover the food," Harry said. "Fair enough?"

"Sure. Frankly, I'd feel safer being here than at my place anyway."

"Deal," Harry said, shaking Gary's hand.

"Well, I'd better go help Jane get our rig loaded," Frank said. He walked back to the coach.

Jane saw him coming as she was unlocking the large storage bin in the rear of the coach.

"How come you went back to the gate?" she asked.

"You didn't see that cut in the razor wire up on the back fence?"

Jane got a scared look on her face. "No. Shit, glad we are getting out of here."

Frank smiled at her. "Me too, but I wouldn't worry too much about this place. They are bringing in reinforcements tonight."

"Who?"

"Hank and Crank," Frank said, snickering. Jane gave him a puzzled look. "Dogs. Big dogs."

"Oh, I get it. Good idea, as long as nobody shoots them."

"Well, enough talk. I need to get busy," Frank said. "I'll load the outside stuff."

"Good. I'm already working on the food. Need to do any checkouts on the rig?"

"I checked the engine fluids before we left her last month, so we should be in good shape there. I'll check the tire pressure. We might want to think about topping off the fresh water."

"We have half a tank," Jane said. "I checked the levels. Holding tanks are empty. The house batteries could use some charging, but the drive will take care of that."

"Alright, let's get busy. I'm a little worried about the roadblock situation."

"Me too, Frank." She picked up a box of food and carried it into the coach as Frank picked up his tool box and loaded it.

"Glad we have this covered spot," Jane said as she came back out to grab another box. "It would be hotter than hell in there if we didn't."

The coach was ready to go in less than an hour.

"I'll back out the coach and get it to the staging area," Frank said. "Follow me out there with the Jeep, and we'll get her hooked up."

Jane nodded. Frank got into the coach and fired up the engine. The Georgetown's V-10 roared to life, and then settled down into a purr. He turned on the rear view camera and checked his mirrors, then slowly backed the coach out of the slanted parking space. He cut hard as his front end cleared the post holding up the carport roof, and then straightened out and drove down the access road. He got to the staging area and straightened out as Jane pulled the Jeep up behind the coach. Frank shut down the engine and went out to do the hook up.

It only took another few minutes to get the Jeep hitched. Jane got in the passenger seat, and Lucy jumped up on her lap. Frank got into the driver's seat.

"Which way are we going, honey?" asked Jane.

"The way I see it, we have three choices. We take I-10 over to I-15 and go north east towards Las Vegas, or we take the I-40 east towards Needles and Bullhead city."

"I think there's going to be a lot of riff-raff on the 15. Maybe on I-40 too," Jane said.

"The other alternative is to take I-10 and make for Quartzsite. We could overnight there and figure out where to go next."

"Boondock, huh? You're brave." Jane said.

"Gotta learn sometime. Wish we had the solar panels, though. One thing about Quartzsite is that we can probably buy solar panels there."

"Alright," Jane said. "I think I-10 is the safest bet. Let's go."

Frank nodded. He started the engine and put the coach in gear, then slowly rolled up to the gate. Harry was outside, moving supplies from his SUV to the office. He waved at Frank, and opened the gate. Frank drove through. Harry trotted over to the driver's side window, and Frank opened it up.

"Good luck, my friend," Harry said.

"You too, Harry. Take care of yourself. Don't get yourself killed over this place."

"I'll try my best. Goodbye, Jane."

"Goodbye, Harry," she said. "Take care."

They drove up to the road, and made a wide right turn. The I-10 onramp was about two miles down. Frank was glad it wasn't further than that. The neighborhood looked as bad as home did. Trash and broken glass littered the sidewalks and the road. He carefully steered the coach through it, trying not to run over anything that would damage the tires. When they were finally rolling down the onramp, Frank sighed with relief.

"Mind if I turn on the radio, Frank?"

"Go ahead. Some news would be good."

Jane got out of her seat and leaned over to turn on the radio. She pushed the button to get to the news station.

"Here's more on that series of sigalerts to the east of the greater Los Angeles area," the announcer said. "The CHP has closed down I-10 eastbound lanes at Ontario due to heavy traffic and a massive multi-car accident."

Jane looked over at Frank, a horrified look on her face.

"I-15 is still open, but getting there is difficult due to the I-10 sigalert and extremely heavy traffic on the 210 freeway."

"Well, at least we are east of that mess on I-10," Jane said.

"I'm glad we left as early as we did."

"You and me both. Wow! Look at that!" Jane pointed to the westbound lanes. It was another military convoy, the biggest one they had seen yet. There was a long line of military trucks rolling along, with CHP cars alongside.

"Are those tanks?" asked Frank. He pointed. There were several massive flatbed trucks with armored vehicles chained to the tops of them. They had gun turrets, but didn't look as big as battle tanks.

All of a sudden the traffic started slowing down quickly, and there were flares on the sides of the road, slowly bringing all the traffic down into just two lanes. Thanks to being so high off the ground, Frank and Jane could see far up ahead. There was a row of

CHP cars and a military truck in the road, ahead about five hundred yards. An officer went up to each car and talked to the driver for a few seconds before letting them through.

"Where did you put the guns?" asked Frank.

"I put them in the drop down bunk above us and closed them in. Unless these folks know this coach, they aren't going to know to look there."

"Smart."

There was shouting up ahead. The CHP officers were pulling people out of a dirty old mini-van that was parked off to the side of the road, past the check point. Somebody yelled "FIREARM", and the CHP officers all drew their weapons and pointed them into the vehicle. Just at that moment several soldiers piled out of the back of the military truck, their weapons at the ready.

"Shit, I hope they don't shut this checkpoint down because of that," Frank said.

Chapter 3 - Goodbye California

"Oh, no," Jane said. Her and Frank watched as one of the CHP cruisers pulled across the two lanes of traffic that were still open, blocking them. The CHP officer at the checkpoint on the left held up his hands to the line of cars waiting, then crouched down behind the CHP Vehicle and pulled his gun, pointing it at the mini-van.

"If anybody starts shooting, get to the back of the coach," Frank said.

"And that means both of us," Jane replied. Frank nodded.

Suddenly there was movement on the far side of the mini-van. The passenger side door opened, and a person ran out, turning and firing a pistol at one of the CHP officers who was running in his direction. The CHP officer dove to the ground.

"Uh oh," Jane said. She undid her seatbelt. "C'mon."

Frank slowly started to unbuckle himself, but kept his eyes on what was unfolding in front of him.

"The army is going to take this one," he said. Jane looked back out just in time to see two of the soldiers step forward and point their assault rifles at the running person. They both fired, and the running person staggered and fell to the ground. There were loud screams coming from inside the mini-van. Then the driver's side door opened, and a pistol was tossed out into the dirt. The driver came out with his hands up. He was an old man, his gray hair blowing in the wind. A CHP officer went cautiously around to the passenger side and slid open the side door. He helped out several people and had them sit over to the side of the vehicle. Then he looked at the other CHP officers and gave a thumbs-up sign.

"Look at that…the people in back are all children," Jane said. "How sad."

"I'll bet the old guy is the father, and he was trying to get his son out of the action. Poor man."

The CHP officer got into the cruiser blocking the two lanes and pulled it out of the way. Then he joined the other officer at the checkpoint, and made a gesture for the next two vehicles to move forward. They went back to the routine; looking, questioning, letting each vehicle go after a minute or two.

"Look, they're bringing up the body," Jane said, pointing. "Good Lord, that's only a kid. Look at him. He looks about sixteen."

"I was afraid of that."

They watched as two soldiers carried the body over next to the military truck. CHP officers were talking to the rest of the people from the mini-van. All of them were crying. Frank got a big lump in his throat. He was fighting back tears. Jane was crying.

"They should have chased down that kid instead of just shooting him like that."

"He had a gun, and was shooting at the officers. The military isn't going to play nice, I'm afraid. Bringing them in is a double-edged sword. Remember Kent State?"

Jane nodded. There were only two vehicles in front of them now.

"If they ask about guns, lie," Frank said.

"Don't you think I know that?"

"Sorry. I'm a little shook up," Frank said.

"No worries, honey."

The car in front of them pulled away, and Frank slowly drove the motor home up to the officer. The butterflies in his stomach were getting out of control. He slid the side window open. Lucy started to bark, but Jane held her close and quieted her down.

"Driver's license, please," the Officer said.

Frank pulled it out and showed it to him through the screen, trying to keep his hands from trembling. The officer looked at it for a couple of seconds, and then nodded.

"That your wife?" he asked.

"Yes."

"Anybody else in the coach?"

"Just a dog and a cat."

"Where are you folks headed?" asked the officer.

"Quartzsite."

"Do you have any firearms? *Say no*."

Frank gave him a puzzled look, and said "No."

"Alright, we'll let you through. Don't stay in Quartzsite too long. Don't go too close to the border. I would suggest going north east."

"Thank you, officer," Frank said. "Take care of yourself." He drove forward, and gave a sigh of relief.

"Geez, I almost peed my pants back there," Jane said.

"You and me both. How about that firearms question? That took me by surprise."

"I know. It's like he had to ask the question, but didn't really want to know."

Frank looked over at her.

"It was more than that. I got a really scary vibe from him. I think he was hoping we were armed. He thinks we need to be armed."

Jane sat silently for a couple of minutes, thinking as she watched the scenery go by.

"There's something that we aren't being told," Jane said. "The state bankruptcy and the problem with the banks is bad enough, but something else is going on."

"Yeah, how about those comments about the border? What the heck was that all about?"

"Exactly," Jane said. "I think we ought to follow the officer's advice. Overnight in Quartzsite. Maybe pick up the solar panels there, and then head up to Utah or Idaho or Wyoming or Montana."

"Agreed. I don't think the Southwest is going to be safe."

"Want a coke, honey?" asked Jane, as she was getting up.

"Sure, sounds good, thanks. I could use a pick-me-up."

Jane went back to the fridge, undid the bungee cord holding the doors shut, and pulled out two cokes. Then she re-attached the bungee cord and started up front. She looked down and noticed the cat carrier under the dinette table.

"Hey, honey, should I let Mr. Wonderful out? He's been in the carrier for a while now."

"Yes. Where's his cat box?"

"I put it in the shower, but I'll pull it out here so we don't have to block the bathroom door open." Jane opened the door of the carrier, and reached in to pet the cat. His head slowly poked out of the door. Then she opened the bathroom door and pulled the cat box out. She put it in front of the dinette.

"No power slides, Frank, or we'll have cat litter all over the place." She laughed. Frank shook his head and snickered as Jane walked back up to the front with the two cokes.

"Yeah, I could see it now. Lucy would go on an Almond Rocca hunt."

"That's disgusting," Jane said, cracking up.

"You know I'm right."

The landscape was getting sparser as they made their way past Cabazon. Soon they were into the Palm Springs area, and there were more buildings. The traffic got heavier. It didn't look like the rioting and looting had come out this far. No litter and broken glass on the streets, at least that you could see from the freeway. No billows of smoke.

"Do we need to stop here?" asked Frank.

"Not on my account. Let me know when you're hungry and I'll get us something."

"Alright. I'm good for now."

After they got past Indio, the landscape transformed into barren desert, and the hills of Chiriaco Summit could be seen in the distance.

"Look, more military coming in," Jane said.

"Wow, look at that. There must be a hundred trucks in this lineup."

"More of those tank things," Jane said, pointing.

"Shit. Those aren't what we saw earlier. Those are battle tanks. Why would they need those?"

Jane looked at him and shook her head.

"What's the difference between these and the earlier ones?"

"Look at the size of the turrets, and the length of the guns. I think the earlier ones were armored personal carriers. Battle tanks are in a whole different category."

"Maybe they're going down to the border."

"Maybe," Frank said. "Or maybe they're being brought in to protect cities. They're overkill for fighting looters, that's for sure. There's definitely something else going on."

Frank could feel the coach slowing down.

"Just about to the Chiriaco grade," Jane said.

"Yep, it'll be hard to talk for a little while. That's the only drawback to these V-10s." Frank gave the rig more gas, and watched the tachometer moving towards four grand. Soon he was back at sixty-five miles per hour. As the climb got steeper, he couldn't hold the speed. He pushed the tow-haul button and felt the engine downshift. It sounded like a tractor.

They got to the summit in about ten minutes, and then started the descent. Frank left the tow-haul button on, letting the engine brake them as they came down from the summit. Soon they were back to flat land, and the engine went back down to its normal cruising rpm.

"You're right, this thing does get noisy when it works that hard," Jane said. "Guess that's why people spend the big bucks for a diesel pusher."

"I guess. This thing has a lot of heart, though. It will run above five grand all day long. I was watching the temp gauge."

"What's that little town up ahead?"

"Desert Center. Really just a wide spot in the road. I remember being in traffic jams there, though, believe it or not."

"Traffic jams out here?" asked Jane.

"Heck yeah, right before the big summer weekends. You go through there to get to Parker and Lake Havasu. Havasu was a zoo on those weekends, big time. Wish we were on that kind of a trip now. Great memories."

"Oh, I get it. You want to go look at all of those college girls taking their tops off," Jane said with a smile on her face.

Frank just looked over at her and grinned.

"How long till we get to Quartzsite?" asked Jane.

"Probably under two hours."

"Good. You want me to drive for a while?"

"I think I'm good for now. Take a nap if you want to. I got to nap in the car earlier."

"Not a bad idea," Jane said. "I'm really tired. What time is it?"

"It's about 2:30."

"If I fall asleep, don't let me sleep past 4:00, OK?"

Frank nodded.

The rest of the drive was non-eventful, except for a few more sightings of military convoys heading towards the coast. Lucy had retreated to her bed, which was behind the passenger seat. Mr. Wonderful made an appearance, slowly walking up between the front seats. He looked like he was going to settle in on the engine cover, but he didn't like the vibration, so he slinked off towards the rear of the coach.

As they were approaching the Arizona border, Frank could see activity. It looked like there was a checkpoint in place on the westbound side of the road, just over the borderline. Assets were being put in place for a checkpoint on the eastbound side, but they weren't going to be done before he got there.

"Jane," Frank said loudly. "Wake up, we're at the Arizona border. You have to see this."

She sat up straight and rubbed her eyes. "What?"

"Check point on the westbound lanes is already set up, and it looks like they're setting one up on the east bound side too."

"Uh oh," Jane said. "They can't stop people from moving across state lines, can they?"

"Not normally, no."

"How much further is Quartzsite?"

"About twenty minutes, I think."

"What time is it now?" she asked.

"About quarter to four. You slept pretty well."

"How are you holding up?"

"Good so far. The drive was easy. I saw more military convoys going west."

"Any more tanks?"

"No, just trucks this time. And no CHP escort like the earlier ones had."

"Goodbye, California," Jane said as they rolled across the border.

The Arizona Hwy Patrol were setting up light bars and barriers. There were cars that said Arizona DPS on them. They looked like CHP vehicles.

"What does DPS stand for?" asked Jane.

"Department of Public Safety, I think."

"Oh. Hungry?"

"I can wait till we get to Quartzsite."

"OK. I'll check out the RV parks on my iPhone. Maybe we'll be lucky and find one with hook-ups for cheap. I don't think this is the best night to try boondocking."

"Agreed," Frank said. "I'm beat. I want to pull in, hook up, and have a drink."

"That sounds good, doesn't it? I see several parks, and they're all in the $25 range. That's a whole lot better than California prices."

"Good, pick a close one."

"There's one a little before Hwy 95," Jane said. "It's five bucks more per night than some of the ones that are further in, but I don't care. It's got good ratings. Exit seventeen. It's coming up. See it?"

"Yep." Frank took the off ramp. They followed the road around, and saw the front gate. Frank pulled in slowly and drove to the staging area. It was a tight fit. There was only room for a couple of rigs, and one was already waiting. He shut off the engine and turned to Jane.

"Want me to go do the honors?"

"No, Frank, you just sit tight and keep Lucy company. You just want one night, right?"

"I think so. I want to see some news. We should be able to add a day or two if we decide it's safe."

"Okay, I'll be back in a few minutes." She got out of her seat and picked up her purse. Then she was out the door. Lucy ran after her, tail wagging.

"Wait, girl," Frank said. "I'll take you out in a minute." He got up out of his seat, and reached for the dog leash. Lucy got excited, jumping up and down and whining. Frank hooked the leash onto her collar and they went out the door and over to the grass median next to the parking area. It was warm, but not as warm as he expected, and a soft breeze blew towards him from the mountains in the distance. Lucy got done with her business quickly, and then went right to sniffing everything in sight. Frank let her lead him around as he looked the place over. There were a lot of coaches there for this time of year. The spaces looked nice.

Jane came walking back out to the coach, a card in her hand. She was shaking her head.

"What?" Frank asked.

“They jacked their price up a little bit. Only by five bucks, but it kind of makes me mad. The people who have the rig parked in front of ours got really mad. I think they're going to leave.”

“Well, opportunity knocks, I guess. So what’s the damage?”

“$35 bucks, plus two bucks each for Lucy and Mr. Wonderful.”

“Oh, well. Who cares? Let’s just get set up and relax for a while. It’s been a hell of a day.”

Jane smiled at him, and they opened the door of their coach. Lucy bounded inside quickly, and got into her bed. Frank got into the driver’s seat, and Jane sat down in the passenger seat.

“Where are we going?” he asked.

“We have space U-15. It’s towards the back. Make a right after the office, then take that road all the way to the back of the park, then veer to the left. We are about half way down that block.”

“Got it.” Frank started the Georgetown and they were off.

The space was nice. There was a good shade tree, a table, and a BBQ. Frank pulled up in front of the entrance and stopped.

“Let’s get the Jeep unhitched.”

"OK," Jane said. They went out into the back. Frank unhooked it, and Jane got behind the wheel and backed it up. She parked on the side of the road, leaving Frank enough room to maneuver. Frank got back into the coach, and pulled it into the space. As Jane was driving the Jeep up next to the coach, she could hear the leveling jacks working, and the coach lurched back and forth until it found level. Frank had the slides out by the time she got through the door.

"Wow, you got done in a hurry!" Jane said as she entered the coach.

"Not done yet…I have to do the hook ups. Be back inside in a minute."

Frank went out and finished up.

"All done now?" asked Jane as Frank walked into the door.

"Almost." He hit the awning button, and it came out, shading the area next to the coach. Then he went out to the back compartment and opened it up. He grabbed two chairs and a table and set them up under the awning. He was just finishing that as Jane walked down the steps.

"Beer, honey?"

"Oh, yeah," he said as he flopped down into one of the chairs.

Jane disappeared back into the coach, and came back with a couple of beers. She sat down, and put one on the table between their chairs.

"Nice out here," Frank said, taking his first sip. He looked out from under their awning. It was late afternoon now, and cooling down nicely. A huge 5th Wheel trailer had just started to back in a couple of spaces down. It was a tight squeeze.

"They're having a little trouble," Jane said.

"I'll go see if another set of eyes will help," he replied, and got up. He walked over to the cab of the truck.

"Need a hand?" Frank asked, smiling.

"That would be great," said the man behind the wheel. "My girlfriend isn't used to this. I can get into the space alright, but I'm worried about those tree branches back there, and I can't see them at all."

"Alright, I'll keep an eye out. Looks like your rear air conditioner housing is going to be a little close. Bring her back slowly."

The man inched backward, while Frank watched up above. When the branch was just about to touch the air conditioner, he put up his hand. The man stopped. He got out of the truck and came around, looking at how close the trailer was going to be to the access road.

"Hmmmmm," the man said. "I like to be a little further back, but this will work. Thanks for the help! I'm Sean." He extended his hand. Frank shook it.

"I'm Frank, and the little lady sitting under the awning over there is my wife, Jane. Good to meet you."

"Sarah, honey, come meet Frank," Sean said, as his girlfriend was walking over. She smiled.

"Good to meet you, Frank," she said, extending her hand. She was an attractive woman in her early thirties, with light brown hair, cut short. Sean walked over beside her. He was about the same age, with very short brown hair, almost in a buzz cut. He looked like military to Frank.

"After you two get situated, come on over and have a beer," said Frank.

"That sounds great, thanks," Sean said. He and Sarah got to work, while Frank walked back over to his chair and sat down.

"Nice couple," Frank said. "Young. Wonder what direction they're coming from?"

"The truck has Arizona plates," Jane said.

"Ahhh, I didn't even notice that. I told them to come over for beer after they were done."

"Good, I'd like to pump them for information."

"Me too."

They watched as the couple finished setting up.

"Looks like more work than a motor home," Jane said.

"It's a routine. Damn, this beer tastes good."

The young couple walked over after about ten minutes. Frank got up and fetched two more chairs from the big rear storage compartment.

"Ready for some beer?" asked Frank as they got under the awning.

"That sounds great," Sean said.

"We have some IPA, also some Coors Banquet, and some other odds and ends."

"Coors would be good," Sean said. "Do you want one, honey?"

"Better not," she said. Then she looked over at Jane. "I'm Sarah. Nice to meet you."

"I'm Jane. Good to meet you too." She got up and went into the coach to get the beers. She brought out two, knowing that Frank would be ready for another one. Everybody sat.

"So, Frank, where are you guys coming from?" asked Sean.

"Southern California, by the coast. An area called South Bay."

"I know where that is. I spent a summer in Hermosa when I was a kid. Nice beaches."

"It's a nice place to live. A little expensive, though," Frank said.

"Where are you guys from?" asked Jane.

"Yuma," Sean said. Sarah looked like she was going to cry, and Sean put his hand on her arm.

"You guys are running away too, I suspect," Jane said.

"Yeah," Sean said.

"It's scary there now," Sarah said.

"Is it as bad in California as they are saying?" asked Sean.

"I think we got out just in time," Frank said.

"Hopefully this will work itself out quickly," Jane said. "The governor called out the National Guard earlier today."

Sean looked over at Frank. He had a grim look on his face.

"Frank, could you give me a hand with something on my trailer?"

"Sure," he replied, getting out of his chair. The two walked over to the 5th wheel.

"You don't really need help with anything, do you?" Frank asked.

"No, I wanted to talk about the situation, but I didn't want to do it in front of Sarah. How's Jane taking all of this?"

“Remarkably well, but she thinks the National Guard is going to get a handle on things in a couple of months.”

“What do you think, Frank?”

“I think M-1 battle tanks are overkill for going after looters.”

“Saw them on the road, did you?”

“Yes. Along with a lot of transport trucks, and a bunch of smaller armored vehicles.”

“Those would be Bradley Fighting Vehicles.”

Frank looked Sean in the eye. There was a lot of concern there.

“You obviously know more about this than I do. You military?”

“Not exactly. I was, but now I’m a civilian employee at the Marine Corps Air Station in Yuma, so I hear a lot of stuff. I guess I should say I *was* an employee. They weren’t happy about me taking off.”

“So what’s happening?” Frank asked.

“It’s bad. And you’re right. You don’t need M-1 battle tanks to take out looters.”

Chapter 4 - Run from the Border

Sarah looked over at their 5th Wheel, as Frank and Sean went around the front to the other side. She sighed.

"What?" asked Jane.

"Sean doesn't need help. He wants to talk to your hubby, where us women folk won't hear. He thinks I'm stupid."

"I hate when they do that."

"Me too, but I know Sean is just trying to keep me from getting too upset."

Jane looked Sarah in the eye like she wanted to say something, but she kept quiet.

"You want to ask me something, don't you? Don't be afraid, Jane."

"You're pregnant, aren't you?"

Sarah gave her a startled look.

"How did you know that? Am I showing already?"

"No, but I can tell. I've always been able to tell. I don't know why. Turning down the beer the way you did helped."

"What way?"

Jane smiled. "Well, 'I'd better not' sounded a little suspicious."

"Oh," Sarah said. She smiled.

"Does Sean know?"

“Of course. I think that’s why he wanted to leave right away.”

“He probably heard things at his job,” Jane said, taking a sip of her beer. “That’s what they're talking about.”

Sarah nodded.

“Don’t worry,” said Jane. “I’ll get them to tell us when they get done with their little conference. I don’t take that coddling crap from my hubby. And he knows it.”

Sarah looked down. She didn’t say anything for a few seconds. Then she looked up.

“I understand what you’re saying, Jane, but I don’t want to make a fuss.”

“Why? Are you afraid of Sean?”

“No, not at all. He’s worried about giving me too much stress this early in the pregnancy. I’m concerned about that too.”

“Alright, then I won’t ask questions. I’m sure Frank will fill me in later. He’s good about that.”

“Thank you, Jane.”

“Here they come,” Jane said. She got up. “You two ready for more beer?”

“That would be great, honey,” Frank said as he walked up. “Maybe an IPA this time.”

“Coming up. How about you, Sean, want to try one of those IPAs?”

"Another Coors would be fine with me. I'm not a big hops fan."

Jane went into the coach to fetch the beers. She came back to silence. She handed out the beers and sat down.

"Lively group," she said.

"It's been a really long day for all of us," Frank said.

"I'll say," Sean added. "Nice to finally get a break."

"How long are you folks going to stay here?" asked Jane. She took a sip of her beer.

Sean looked over at Sarah.

"Don't know," he said. He watched Sarah for a reaction.

"I'll go along with whatever you think is safest, Sean. You know that."

"Okay. I just don't…"

"Sean, Jane knows," Sarah said. "She figured it out on her own, so no need to tiptoe around."

Sean got an embarrassed look on his face.

"Okay, what did I miss?" asked Frank.

"Sarah is pregnant, dummy," Jane said. She enjoyed Frank's shocked look.

"Ohhhhhh," he said. "That puts a new spin on things."

"Sorry, Frank," Sean said. "I didn't want to tell you that until I asked Sarah first."

"Hey, no problem at all, Sean. We've only just met, you know."

"I know."

"It's getting a little noisy all of a sudden," Jane said. She stood up to try to find out what the commotion was about. "Oh, shit, look at that."

Frank stood up and looked in the direction that Jane was looking. There was a big lineup of RVs parked at the gate.

"Wow. I guess we'll have to get out of here tomorrow, or we'll pay a lot more than 35 bucks."

Sean looked up at Frank and shook his head, smiling.

"What, 35 bucks? They charged us 45 bucks. I think you guys were here about half an hour before we showed up. Highway robbery."

Frank and Sean looked at each other and started cracking up.

"Well, if that officer at the checkpoint was right, they have to make it while they can," Jane said.

Sarah looked over at Jane, her brow furrowed. "What checkpoint?"

"There was a checkpoint in California that we had to go through," Frank said. "The officer that talked to us there said not to stay in Quartzsite too long, and not to go near the border. He said to go north east."

Sarah shot a worried glance over at Sean.

"Maybe we should change the subject," Jane said, looking over at Frank.

"Or maybe we should hit the sack and try to get up early tomorrow," Frank said. "We're all tired, and tomorrow's going to be another long day, I suspect."

"That suits me," Sean said. He looked relieved.

"Me too," Sarah said. "Thanks so much for helping us today."

"And thanks for the beers, too," Sean said. "The next rounds are on us." The young couple got up.

Frank stood up and shook hands with Sean.

"OK, you two, have a nice night," Jane said, getting up. The young couple walked back to their trailer, hand in hand.

"I'm going to lock this stuff up before it gets dark," Frank said, folding up his chair. Jane nodded and folded her chair up. Frank took those two back to the storage compartment and put them in. When he got back under the awning, Jane had already folded up the other two chairs. Frank took those to the storage compartment, and Jane picked up the table and brought it over too.

Frank locked it up, and turned to Jane. He put his arm around her lower waist and pulled her close. She started a soft sobbing. He patted her back.

"C'mon, honey, let's go inside. It's getting dark."

Jane nodded, and they got into the coach. Frank pushed the button to pull in the awning.

"Another beer, honey?" Jane asked.

"No, I want to have a clear head in the morning." He sat down at the dinette. She joined him.

"Alright, let's have it. What was your little pow-wow about?" asked Jane.

"Rumors, mostly. Not sure how much of it I believe."

"Go on."

"You know that terror group that just took over a big part of Iraq?"

"Yes, of course."

"According to the rumors, they've been sending soldiers into Mexico via Venezuela, to organize border incursions into the southwestern United States."

"Why would they do that? They can't win."

"Well, here's where I take this with a grain of salt. Sean thinks our government is in on this deal, and they are going to use it to declare martial law and suspend our rights."

"Oh, brother. Another one of those," Jane said, "and they're going to do this because?"

"He says it's because of the global warming thing. He says it's the only way the Feds have to 'force' people to make the lifestyle changes required to combat climate change."

"He probably brought up Agenda 21 too, huh? Nutcase."

Frank just shook his head.

"Well, not exactly. You and I don't agree about Global Warming, but let's not dive down into that rabbit hole for now. Let's just focus on what we do know and what we can see. People tend to draw a lot of far out conclusions to fit their narrative. That isn't helpful."

"Agreed," Jane said. She had a sly smile on her face.

"Here's what I believe is possible, maybe even probable. I know that the terrorists are getting ready to start pushing on us again. I believe that they very well may be out to cause some problems along the border, and I could see Venezuela lending a hand."

"You think this is plausible because?"

"Remember those battle tanks we saw earlier?"

"Yeah," she said. "OK, you have my attention."

"It's also obvious to me that California has been targeted. I don't believe that all of the problems going on there are due to a bunch of kids looting after a financial crisis. Hell, all of our money is still in our accounts. Same with most people, I suspect. Somebody is whipping this up. Maybe we have an alliance going on between some bad folks south of the border and those cretins in the Middle East."

"Ok, I'll grant you that what's going on in California is more complex than we're being told. So what are we going to do with this information?"

"I think we ought to do exactly what we were planning to do before we met these kids. I think we ought to leave tomorrow and drive north. And we should keep going until we're in the upper plains states, or the upper Midwest."

"Well, that should make for an interesting winter, but I'm with you."

"One other thing," Frank said. He was silent for a moment, and looked down at the table. "Sean asked if they could tag along with us."

"I'm not sure I'm OK with that," Jane said. "He sounds a little on the nutty side to me, and I don't want to get all tied up with their pregnancy."

"I know, me neither. But I don't want to confront them right off the bat. We're both going in the same direction anyway. Why don't we just let them follow us for now, and play it by ear?"

"Alright, but let's keep our distance."

"Agreed."

Frank got up and went over to the couch. He picked up the remote and turned the TV on. The reception was poor.

"Shoot, nothing on the antenna. This place doesn't have cable, does it?"

"Sorry, Frank, I forgot to check before we picked this place."

Frank went to the local channel that came in the best. It was showing the network affiliate's sitcoms.

"How about WiFi?" asked Frank.

"I've been trying to get on for the last couple of hours…pretty much every time I came into the coach since we've been here. No dice. I have bars, but I can't connect to the internet."

"Shit," Frank said. "I wanted to be able to check out the condo."

"I know, me too."

"Radio?"

"I don't know, let's see." Jane went up to the front of the coach and turned the ignition switch on. Then she turned on the radio and hit the seek button. It took a few tries, but she found a news station.

"I-10, I-40, and I-15 have all been shut down, both east and west bound, in order to better lock down the area during this crisis," the announcer said. "Some alternate routes are still open between California and the Arizona and Nevada borders, but they will likely be shut down in the coming hours."

Jane looked over at Frank, who was staring up towards the front of the coach.

"What crisis are they talking about?" asked Frank.

Jane just looked over at him and shook her head.

"Now here's the latest on the border crisis," the announcer said. "Border skirmishes have been increasing between Chula Vista and El Centro, with the US Army now getting directly involved. This after the airliner was shot down while taking off from San Diego's Lindbergh Field several hours ago, killing all aboard."

"Oh, my God," Jane said.

"Fighter jets and helicopter gunships from nearby bases have been dispatched to the area, and are engaging the insurgents. The Mexican government has had no comments so

far, and in fact it is likely that the Mexican government is no longer in place. The Administration is currently trying to ascertain who is leading the border incursions, and have scheduled a press conference for early tomorrow morning. At this time there has been no action against Mexico other than attacks on the forces coming over the border."

"Well, at least part of what Sean was saying appears to be true," Frank said. He pulled out the AAA Road Atlas and opened it up to the big map of the US.

"How far are we from the border right now?"

"According to the map, we are about as far as Temecula is from the border in California. A ways, but not far enough to stay here, that's for sure."

"Should we leave tonight?"

"No, we're too tired, but let's hit the sack and be up before 6:00 tomorrow morning."

"Alright, honey, let's go to bed," she said, switching off the radio.

They turned out the lights in the coach, and went into the bedroom. They got their PJs on and were just laying down when they heard Lucy run in.

"Mind if she comes up?" asked Jane.

"No, it's fine."

"C'mon, girl, jump up," said Jane. Lucy bounded up onto the bed. She sniffed and nuzzled both Jane and Frank, and then laid down between them with a sigh. They all drifted off to sleep.

Frank awoke with a start. Mr. Wonderful had gotten up on the bed, and was purring loudly, his nose touching the side of Frank's face.

"Thanks a lot," Frank said.

"What's wrong, honey?"

"Mr. Wonderful just woke me up."

"So what else is new? Go back to sleep."

Frank tried to get back to sleep, but he couldn't. He checked the time on his cellphone. It said 5:30. He decided to get up, and went quietly to the kitchen counter to turn on the coffee machine. He picked out one of the bold coffee pods and brewed it. Jane came out just as his cup was full.

"That one for me?" she asked, smiling.

"It's bold. Do you want it, or should I make you one of the mild ones?"

"Mild. I'll do it. Go ahead and enjoy your cup."

Frank nodded and carried his coffee cup over to the dinette. He raised the blind on the window and looked out. Sean was already up, getting his rig ready to go.

Jane sat down with her cup, and looked out the window.

"Well, they aren't sleeping in, are they?"

"Nope. I suspect we'll get a knock on the door any time now."

"Just go about your business, Frank."

"Alright." He finished his cup, and then went into the bedroom to get dressed.

He came back out, and looked out the window again. There were other people getting ready to leave.

"Hey, honey, will you take care of Lucy's walk while I'm getting things unhooked?" Frank asked.

"Sure, no problem." She got up to get dressed.

Frank opened the door of the coach and stepped out into the cool morning. There was a flyer taped to the door on the outside. Frank pulled it off and looked at it. Then he laughed. He opened the door back up.

"Jane, guess what?"

"What?"

"We got a flyer from the park management taped to our door. It says that if we want to stay another night, it's 150 bucks, and it says that if we aren't out before 9:00am, they are going to charge an extra fee."

"Bullshit," Jane said. "The contract I signed said checkout time was 11:00 am."

"Who cares? We'll be out of here by 7:30 if not sooner."

"True. I'm coming out with Lucy."

"Okay. I'm going to go ahead and bring the slides in when you guys are out. Then I'll finish unhooking. I think I'll fill the fresh water tank too."

"Good idea," she said as she came down the steps with Lucy in front of her.

Frank brought in the slides and got the jacks up, then got up and looked around the coach. Not much to stow. They didn't get much out last night. He went outside and got the utilities unhooked. He was back in the coach raising the front blinds when Jane walked up with Lucy.

"Mission accomplished," Jane said.

"Good. Go ahead and get the fridge buttoned up. I'll pull out on the road so we can hook up the Jeep."

"Got it. You want anything to eat?"

"I'm not hungry at this point. Why don't you put that box of Clif Bars up in the front?"

"Sounds like a plan."

Frank got the coach pulled out on the access road, and hooked up the Jeep into place behind it. As he was finishing, Sean walked up.

"Well, Frank, we're ready to go."

"Headed to Flagstaff?"

"Yep, for now. You?"

"Yeah, same," replied Frank. "How good a road is Route 60?"

"It's not terrible. If you're going to Flagstaff, you'll have to switch over to Route 71 and then Route 89. They aren't great, but good enough."

"Alright, thanks," Frank said, walking over and shaking hands with Sean. "Good luck to you. Maybe we'll see you in Flagstaff."

"Hopefully," said Sean. He turned and walked over to his truck. Frank watched as they slowly drove to the front gate.

Frank got into the coach. Jane was already sitting in the passenger seat. Frank got into the driver's seat and started the engine.

"Sean going the same way we are?"

"Yes. It's the only way you can go, I'm afraid."

Jane nodded. Frank put the coach in gear and drove to the gate. There was a huge lineup of rigs there. People were bickering at each other. There was a big sign on the door that had the new prices listed.

"Geez, people are starting to get panicky," Jane said.

"If I was the owner of this park, I'd put a limit on this price gouging. If the customers get mad enough, there's going to be problems, and I doubt that the local authorities are going to want to get involved."

As they passed through the gate and onto the street, a gunshot startled both of them. Frank looked into his side mirror and saw several men running into the office.

"That didn't sound good. What happened?" Jane asked.

"Looks to me like some customers have already gotten tired of the prices," Frank said. "I'm so glad we are getting out of here."

Route 60 was not built to handle the volume it was getting. It was moving, but only at about 30 mph. A mixture of cars, big rigs, and RVs were on the road as far up as Frank could see. It was bad all the way to Route 71, where Route 60 heads off to Phoenix and Route 71 heads north. Most of the people on the road were going to Phoenix, and that helped a lot. Frank could see Sean and Sarah's 5th wheel ahead of them in the distance as they got on 71. The traffic sped up to about 55 mph.

"Whew, glad to be out of that," Jane said. "Want a Clif bar?"

"Sure, good idea. Wish we could make coffee on the road."

Jane nodded, and handed a bar over to Frank. He tore open the wrapper and devoured it quickly, washing it down with the bottle of water that Jane had put in his cup holder. Jane ate a bar as well.

Suddenly Frank saw flashing lights in his rear-view mirrors.

"Oh, shit, what now?" he said.

"What?"

"Can't see yet, but it looks like we have some emergency or police vehicles coming up behind us in a hurry."

"Do you need to pull over?"

"No, there isn't much in the way of southbound traffic. They've been passing to the left."

The vehicles were upon them in seconds, passing them on the left at a fast clip. It was two Arizona DPS cruisers, and an army Humvee with a gun mounted in the back.

"Uh oh, I don't like the look of that," Jane said.

"Me neither," Frank said.

Jane sat up higher in her seat and pointed, a panicked look on her face.

"Shit, look, they're pulling over Sean and Sarah's rig!"

Chapter 5 - Protests and Arrests

Jane moved her head around until she could see behind the coach using the passenger side mirror.

"Look at that," she said, her voice wavering.

Frank looked in his mirror, just in time to see the two soldiers pointing their assault rifles into Sean's truck.

"Oh no, I don't believe it," Frank said.

"Should we stop?"

"No way. And turn off your cellphone."

"Off? Why?" Jane asked.

"What if they ask Sean who he's talked to?"

"Shit. Alright."

Frank fished his cellphone out of his pocket and tossed it to Jane.

"Take the back off mine and remove the battery."

Jane nodded. She had a horrified look on her face, and kept looking into the mirror every few seconds.

"I can't see them anymore," she said.

"Me neither. I wish you didn't have an iPhone. Can't take the batteries out of those."

"Turning it off won't do the trick?"

"It's supposed to, but I read an article a while back that said the iPhone was still traceable even when it is turned off."

Jane looked out the window, watching the scenery go by, and thinking.

"I'll toss it out the window if you want me to," she said.

Frank thought about it for a moment.

"No, let's not do that. I'm probably panicking too much. Did you tell either of them your last name? I didn't."

"No, I never did. I paid cash for the space in that park, too."

"Good," Frank said. "Did you put our name on a register?"

"No, they didn't ask me too, but those people were nervous. They just got done with a shouting match when I walked in. We lucked out."

"We're probably alright, then. Maybe we should go somewhere other than Flagstaff, though."

"I'll go get the road atlas." Jane got up and went into the back.

Lucy got out of her bed and followed Jane, tail wagging. Jane was back up in her seat in a couple of minutes. Lucy jumped in her lap.

"Doesn't look like Lucy is going to let you open that road atlas," Frank said, laughing.

"I can wait a little bit. We'll be on this road for a while, and as I remember, it basically turns into Route 89."

"Alright."

They were silent for a little while, as they watched the desert flow by. The road had thinned out nicely, allowing them to drive at 65 mph. Lucy finally got tired of sitting on Jane's lap and got down into her bed.

"So what do you think happened back there?" asked Jane.

"I'm not sure. If we believe what Sean was saying, maybe he got picked up because they were afraid he was going to talk."

"Been thinking that."

"But on the other hand, I'm not sure about Sean. He wasn't exactly being honest with me. Leaving out Sarah's pregnancy was a big one, frankly."

"If he isn't honest, then what do you think that was about?"

"Maybe he's really still in the service, and he went AWOL. Look at that haircut. Or maybe he stole some stuff on the way out. Maybe he did something bad to somebody back there. Who knows? We really didn't know him at all."

"Well, you know how I feel about anti-government conspiracy nuts, Frank. But this worries me. Crazy things are happening right now, and they sent two Arizona trooper's vehicles and an Army Humvee off to nab this one guy? Something isn't right."

Frank was silent again, thinking, running over Sean's story in his mind. He looked over at Jane.

"Maybe tonight would be a good time to try boondocking. I think we should stay off the grid for a day or two and watch."

"I was thinking the same thing," Jane said. She picked up the road atlas and opened it up to the Arizona page. "How about Williams? I remember reading that a lot of people boondock there when they go to the Grand Canyon."

"Where is it?"

"Right where Route 89 hits I-40."

"Hmmmmm. I-40 is an awful big road."

"That might not be a bad thing in this case," Jane said. "If we're lucky, there will be a whole lot of people boondocking there, and we'll just disappear into the crowd."

"Make's sense. Let's do it."

"Alright. Thirsty? Want a coke?"

"Yes, that would be great, thanks."

Jane got up and went to the fridge to fetch them. She was back in her seat fast.

"Frank, mind if I turn on the radio? Maybe we can get some more news."

"Go ahead."

Jane reached over and switched the radio on, using the seek button again to find a station.

"Here we go," Jane said. She turned up the radio.

"People in the greater Los Angeles area have been advised to stay indoors," the announcer said. "Looting is now going on in the daylight hours, and the police don't have the resources to stop it. There are a growing number of reports now that private citizens are protecting their property and themselves with firearms. Local authorities have been warning citizens that using deadly force to protect property alone is illegal. Only protection of yourself or others with deadly force is allowed by law."

"When we can make a phone call, I'm going to call Robbie and tell him to go get the guns out of our safe," Frank said.

"If they're still there."

Frank nodded.

"All of the towns along the Mexican border in California are now under Martial Law," the announcer continued. "Citizens are being evacuated from those areas as the army

moves in. Last night, border skirmishes moved eastward into Arizona. They were stopped just east of Yuma, at the Barry M Goldwater Air Force Range, which extends eastward along the border for many miles."

Frank laughed.

"Yes, go ahead and mess with an Air Force base, you idiots," he said.

Jane looked over at him and shook her head.

"Well, at least you're happy about something."

"Meanwhile, in Washington, protesters have staged large rallies, telling the Administration that people coming over the border are refugees, not an invading army. Counter protests arose quickly, resulting in violence and many arrests. The Administration promised a press conference yesterday, but then rescheduled for tomorrow morning. The Administration has been very quiet about this crisis thus far."

"I hope this mess doesn't give the reactionaries a chance to get a foothold," Jane said.

"Seriously? You still think that anybody right of center is racist? Look at what we're seeing. These aren't refugees coming over the border."

"We don't know what they are yet," Jane said. "But I'll admit I'm not buying the refugee story at this point. I think everybody needs to cool their jets for a little while. Us included."

"Look up ahead!" Frank said. "That's a lot of cops coming this way."

Jane looked up and could see the flashing lights. It was a whole line of police cars, but they didn't have the usual DPS insignia.

"Those look like local cops," she said.

Now they were upon them, and the coach rocked as they flew past.

Jane reached over and switched off the radio. "Mind?"

"No, it's just going to get us chewing on each other. Sorry, sweetie."

"Me too."

The rest of the drive was uneventful, and soon they were at the I-40 junction. Williams was up ahead just a few miles.

"Better see if you can find us a place."

"Boy, I sure miss my iPhone now," Jane said.

"We have that camping guide in the back, maybe we should look at that."

"Alright, I'll go dig it out."

Frank nodded.

Jane went to the rear of the coach for a few minutes, and then made her way back to her seat with a paperback. She flipped to the central Arizona section.

"Wow, there's a lot here," she said. "We should check out Dogtown."

"How do I get there?"

"Get off of I-40 in Williams, and then take 4th street south about 4 miles. Then make a left on Dogtown Road. The book says that there's camping on either side of that road, and it's completely free."

Frank got off I-40 and found 4th street quickly.

"More rigs around here," Frank said. "That's good."

"Yeah, and this road is a little better than I expected. Pretty, too. I didn't expect all of the pine trees."

4th street was paved, but small. Every so often there was a dirt road going off to the right or the left. Dogtown Road wasn't hard to find. It was large for a dirt road. They made the left, and drove slowly.

"Look, there are some people camped over to the left," Jane said, pointing.

"Looks pretty level, but there's probably something with more room open up ahead," Frank said.

They continued down the road, and the number of coaches did thin out a little bit. Finally they came to a spot that was large and level, and there weren't any coaches there yet.

"How does that look?" asked Frank.

"Looks like it will do nicely. Let's take it, but I'd pull in a ways. I suspect we'll have company before long."

"OK," Frank said. He turned onto the dirt and drove towards the back of the clearing. He stopped.

"Aren't you going back a little further?"

"We have to unhook the TOAD before I can back in."

"Oh, yeah," said Jane. "Forgot it was back there."

Frank shut off the engine, and got out of his seat.

"I'll take Miss Lucy out," Jane said. "I'm sure she could use a pit stop."

Frank nodded. He opened the door of the coach. The air was fresh and clean, like mountain air. It was much cooler than Quartzsite had been. The smell of the pine trees hit him, and he savored it. He walked around to the back of the coach and unhitched the Jeep. Jane was letting Lucy drag her all over the clearing, sniffing the ground every few seconds, her tail wagging.

Frank backed the Jeep off, and then drove it over next to the stand of trees that was the back boundary of the clearing. He stowed the tow bar in the back compartment, and waited for Jane to finish up with Lucy. The two came walking up after a few minutes.

"I'm thinking that we back the coach up next to where I've got the Jeep parked. That way, if we have to leave quickly, we can just pull forward."

"Good idea. Got to watch those tree branches up there, though. Some of them look a little low."

"That's why I waited for you," Frank said, smiling. He went into the coach and fired up the engine. Then he made a wide turn back towards the road, and put the coach into reverse. He slid open his side window so he could hear Jane, and backed up, slowing as he saw the trees getting closer.

"Just about two more feet," Jane shouted. Frank backed up a little more, and then put the coach into park and shut off the engine.

"Aren't you going to level?" asked Jane.

"I want to put those blocks under the jacks first," he said. "I don't want them sinking into the dirt. It's a little soft."

Jane nodded, and followed Frank to one of the side storage compartments. She helped him get out the blocks and carry them around to all four jack locations. After they were all placed under the jacks, Frank got back into the coach, and did the leveling and the slides. Jane came inside afterwards, with Lucy bouncing along behind her.

"Want some coffee?" she asked.

"I've got a better idea. There's a Starbucks in Williams. It's only about five miles away. I say we grab the laptop and go over there. I want to see what's going on in the house, and I want to try to get ahold of Robbie."

"Good plan. Should we take Lucy?"

"I think we ought to leave her in the coach. Her bark sounds bigger than she is, and there's nobody to bother around here. We'll only be gone for a little while."

"Okay, let's go."

The two of them checked out the windows to make sure they were locked, and Frank lowered the blinds in the front of the coach. He got out and locked up the storage compartments. After Jane climbed out, he locked the coach door. Then he met her by the Jeep. She was holding the laptop case.

"Why don't I drive?" she said. "You've driven enough today."

"Sounds great, honey." They got into the car and pulled away.

"This is such pretty country," Jane said as she drove along. They were at 4th street in minutes, and then they sped up.

"Look, two more coaches coming in," Frank said, pointing ahead of them. "We might have neighbors by the time we get back."

"Could be. Where was the Starbucks?"

"We passed it when we got off I-40. I think that road was old Route 66."

"Really? I didn't notice that."

They saw two more coaches making their way south on 4th Street before they got into Williams. It didn't take long to find the Starbucks. The parking lot was about half full. Jane found a spot, and they parked. Frank picked up the laptop, and they walked to the door.

There were still tables open, so Frank sat down on one by the window and set up the laptop. There was an electrical outlet close enough.

"Excellent," Frank said.

"What do you want? I'll go order."

"I want a Grande Pike and a couple of Old Fashioned donuts, if they have them.

"Alright, be back in a second."

Frank turned on the laptop, and it started its boot up. While it was working, he looked around. Most of the people looked like locals. Flannel shirts, jeans, work boots. A couple of police officers came in, talking to each other in hushed tones as they approached the cashier. There were several college kids sitting at a large table in the back, having a slightly loud political discussion, but laughing and joking at the same time. They struck Frank as being very nervous. The kids took notice when the police officers looked their way, and got quiet.

"Here you go," Jane said, setting the coffee cup and a bag down on the table next to the laptop.

"Outstanding," Frank said. He quickly picked up the cup of coffee and had a sip. "Been waiting for that."

Jane sat down on the chair facing Frank and had a sip of her coffee as well. She pulled a Cheese Danish out of her bag and started eating.

Frank logged onto the laptop and got it connected to the Wi-Fi. It was slow, but it worked.

"Anything?"

"Not yet. Checking e-mail first, to see if either of the kids have sent us anything.

"Good idea. I'm coming around to that side of the table." Jane dragged her chair over, and

Frank moved closer to the window to give her some room.

"Here's something from our girl," Frank said. He opened it. "She's just asking where we went. I'm going to reply and tell her we're fine, but I'm not going to say where we are."

"Alright. I'm glad she's up in Oregon."

"Me too."

Frank wrote the reply and sent it. Then he pulled one of his donuts out and devoured it in about three bites.

"Hungry, I guess," Jane said with a playful grin.

"You're making pretty good progress there yourself."

Jane looked at him, then pulled him close and kissed him gently.

"I'm glad we have each other," she said.

"Me too."

Frank reached for his wallet and brought it up. He pulled out a slip of paper.

"What's that?" Jane asked.

"The IP address of our security cameras."

"Oh."

Frank opened a new browser window and input the IP address. It opened up to a console. He selected camera number one, which showed the front of their condo and the driveway.

"Oh crap," he said, leaning back in his chair.

"What?"

"Look. There's a whole line of cars in our driveway."

"Oh no."

"We'd better call Robbie. I don't want him going near the place."

"I'll turn on my iPhone," Jane said. She reached into her purse and pulled it out.

"There are several young men sitting in our living room," Frank said as he looked at camera number 2.

Jane's phone was back on line, so she dialed Robbie. She heard the ringer start up. Then a click.

"Mom?" said the worried voice on the other end.

"Yes, honey, it's me. We're alright."

"Where are you guys?"

"We can't tell you on the phone. I'll explain it to you later. We are north east of where you are. We're in a safe place."

"Alright, I understand, mom," Robbie said.

"We need to warn you about something…"

"Wait a minute," said Frank. He was staring at a picture of the garage.

Chapter 6 - Boondocking in the Pines

"What do you see in the garage, Frank?" asked Jane, a scared look on her face. People in the Starbucks were noticing her distress. The place got quiet.

"Look - Robbie's car," Frank said.

Jane looked relieved.

"Robbie, you're at our house?" asked Jane.

There was silence on the line for a moment.

"Yes, Mom. I'm sorry," Robbie said. "We had to leave the apartment."

"Oh, honey, I'm not upset that you're there," Jane said. "I'm relieved. You don't know how worried I've been about you."

"So Robbie and his friends are at our house?" asked Frank.

"Yes, Frank."

"Good. Let me talk to him for a minute."

"Robbie, your father wants to talk to you," Jane said. "Don't worry, he's glad you're there, too."

"Alright, mom."

Frank took the phone from Jane.

"Hi, son. Are you safe?"

"Hi, dad. I think we're safer here. I brought some of my friends over."

"I can see them in the video," Frank said. "That's fine. Do you trust all of them?"

"Yes, of course, dad. You've met a couple of them."

"How many do you have there?"

"Three," Robbie said.

"What's been going on around there?"

"Bad stuff. A gang attacked our apartment complex yesterday. I got out with Steve and Gil. We didn't know where else to go, so we came over here."

"Anybody get hurt?"

"No. Gil had his hunting rifle. The gang tried to stop us from driving off, but when he pointed the gun at them, they got out of the way."

"Good."

"There were some problems here, too. Some thugs attacked the front unit yesterday. Rick and Diane got away, but the gang ransacked the place. Then they tried to get into the middle unit. Nobody was home, but they couldn't get the door open. We had our cars in the driveway blocking your unit. The way we parked, you can barely get past in the front. They tried to come around the back. I think one of them broke his shoulder trying to break in the back-garage door. Nice job with that 4 X 4, by the way."

Frank snickered.

“Good, glad it held. What are you planning to do?”

“Well, hang out for a while, if that’s alright with you. My job is shut down for now.”

“How many guns do you guys have?”

“Gil has his 30-30 Marlin lever gun. That’s it. And he’s only got about fifteen rounds of ammo.”

“Alright. Get a piece of paper and a pencil.”

“Just a sec,” Robbie said. He put down the phone, and left for a moment. “OK, got it.”

“Here’s the combo to the gun safe. It’s in the closet in the master, behind some clothes. Combo is left 35 right 12 left 8.”

“Got it. What’s in there?”

“Another 30-30 and about two hundred rounds of ammo, plus two Weatherby bolt action hunting rifles with scopes and about twenty rounds of ammo for each, a couple of hand guns, and a double barrel shot gun with about fifty shells. Not sure how much pistol ammo there is in there…I took a lot of it when we left.”

“Thanks, dad. We’ll hang out and protect your place,” Robbie said.

“I’m not worried about the condo. Protect yourself, son.”

“Where are you guys? When are you coming home?”

"We're in another state to the east, in the motor home. We got out of California just before they got it locked down. I don't know when we are coming home. It may be a while."

"I wish I was out of here too. I've been hearing bad stories about the army. They'll shoot you if they even think you're looting now."

"Seen any tanks around town?"

"I've seen them on the freeway, but they were all going south."

"Alright, Robbie, you take care of yourself. I love you. I'll give you back to mom."

"Love you too, dad," Robbie said. Frank handed the phone back to Jane.

"Robbie, there's quite a bit of food in the deep freeze," Jane said. "Use it."

"OK, mom. We'll do that. We were able to bring quite a bit of food with us. We're OK for a week or so just on that."

"Alright, honey. Be careful. Avoid the soldiers if you can."

"I'll try, mom. I love you."

"I love you too, Robbie," Jane said. Her eyes were misting. "We'll be in touch."

"Bye."

Jane put the phone back on the table, looked over at Frank, and put her hand on his.

"Robbie is probably going to be fine, honey," Frank said. "They'll have to make a food run eventually, but we did leave the place pretty well stocked."

"Yep, there's even a couple of turkeys in the deep freeze, and a lot of fish."

Frank looked at some news on the internet.

"Lots of heated rhetoric going on. Looking at Drudge."

"I suppose they're making the Administration look like absolute beasts," Jane said.

"Pretty much, but Slate is saying that the Tea Party is behind the whole thing, so there's plenty of BS to go around."

Jane shook her head.

"I think we should be getting back," she said.

"Agreed, but order me a refill. This coffee tastes great."

"OK, sweetie," Jane said. She got up and walked to the counter with Frank's cup as he shut down the laptop.

Soon they were back in the jeep, with Frank driving this time. There was more traffic in town now, and on 4th street. They saw another four or five rigs behind them as they made the left turn onto Dogtown Road. It didn't take long to get back to their clearing. There were two other coaches there, on either side of their rig, widely spaced. Frank pulled the Jeep up next to their coach, and he and Jane got out.

"I figured we'd have company," Jane said, as she unlocked the door to the coach and opened it. Lucy bounded out, tail wagging.

"Hi, girl," Frank said, squatting down to pet her as she licked his hands and arms.

"You want a drink, Frank?"

"Not yet, still working on this coffee," he replied. "I'll get the chairs out and get the awning set up."

"Sounds like a great idea."

Frank went to the back compartment and pulled out all four chairs, figuring that they'd have company eventually. He also pulled out the table, and set them all up next to the coach. Then he reached into the door and hit the awning button, and it extended itself.

Frank was just sitting down as Jane came back out of the coach. She sat down on the chair next to him, and Lucy jumped up on her lap.

"How's Mr. Wonderful doing?" Frank asked.

"He's still hiding somewhere. I think we need to make sure we keep the screen door latched, or we'll lose him."

Frank nodded.

"How long do you think we'll be able to run the fridge before we have to fire up the generator?" asked Jane

"I'm hoping we can make it through to tomorrow morning, but we'll have to keep an eye on the battery level."

"Too bad we couldn't get solar before we left Quartzsite."

"Well, at least we're all in the same boat here, so we shouldn't get a lot of crap for running the generator."

"How much gas do we have left?" asked Jane.

"We're good. Over thrce quarters of a tank. We'll want to top it off in town before we leave, though."

Frank saw two people walking in their direction from the coach on the left. It was a couple about their age. Both of them were a little overweight. The man had a large white beard, giving him a Santa Claus look. The woman wore tailored clothes and looked attractive for her age. She had a pretty round face, and shoulder length black hair with streaks of gray starting to show.

"Hi there," Frank said, standing up and extending his hand. "I'm Frank, and this is Jane."

“Very pleased to meet you,” said the man. “I’m Hank, and this is Linda.”

Jane stood up now too. “Pleased to meet you both,” she said.

“Have a seat,” Frank said, motioning at the two extra chairs.

“Thanks,” Hank said. The couple sat down.

“So, where are you folks coming from?” asked Frank.

“San Diego,” Hank said. Linda nodded. “You?”

“Redondo Beach,” Frank said. “You were in a worse place than we were, from the sound of it.”

“We got out a week ago,” Hank said. “We were hoping that Quartzsite would be far enough away. Wrong.”

“Yes, we just came from there,” Jane said. “Some shooting started up as we were leaving the park.”

“Wait a minute, were you guys at the place right by highway 95?”

“Yes,” Frank said. “Why?”

“There was a riot there, and the military rolled in. About thirty people got killed.”

“No, really?” asked Jane.

“Really. That’s what put us over the edge to get the hell out of there.”

"We aren't settling down again until we are up to Montana," Linda said. "Snow or no snow." She laughed heartily.

"We aren't sure how far we'll go up yet," Frank said. He took the last drink of his coffee, and put the cup down on the table.

"Ahh, you guys went to the Starbucks in town," Hank said. "We are fixin to do that. I want to use their Wi-Fi."

"That's the main reason we went," Jane said. "We wanted to check on our son and our house."

"How are things there now?" asked Linda.

"Worse than they were when we left," Jane replied. "Our son is holed up in our condo. It's in a better neighborhood than where he was living."

"That's good," Hank said. "We don't have any kids, so at least we don't have that worry."

"Any news from your place?" asked Frank.

"Not really, other than what we've heard on the news. You heard about the plane getting shot down, right?"

"Yes, heard that on the radio."

"We decided to leave a few days before that happened, because of the types of immigrants we started seeing around town," Hank said. "Not your usual wetbacks."

"Hank, don't say things like that," said Linda. She looked over at Frank and Jane. "Sorry."

"No worries," said Frank.

"Anyway, they don't look like the usual peasants that come over the border illegally," Hank said. He looked at Linda. "Better?"

"Yes, thank you," she said.

Jane smirked and looked over at Frank.

"How so?" asked Frank.

"They were better looking specimens, frankly. They looked like soldiers, and carried themselves like soldiers. Also the usual immigrant women and children seemed to be gone all of a sudden."

"Tell them about the others," Linda said.

"Others?" Jane asked.

"Yeah, I saw a few men around who didn't quite look Mexican. They had dark hair and dark skin, but they were different somehow. Then I heard a couple of them speaking in a different language. Sounded like Arabic to me."

"Shit, I knew it," Frank said. "Our government wouldn't do anything about the borders, and now this."

Jane put her hand on his arm and looked him in the eye, trying to get him to calm down.

"Go on," she said.

"There's really not much else to tell. The looting had been going on at night, just like up your way, but we were ready to ride that out at first. We have a condo in a high rise down by the water, and it's well guarded and secured on the ground floor, so we weren't having problems. What pushed us to leave were the others I was just talking about. It started to seem very dangerous there. It was more than just a few disgruntled people looting. More than just rioting. I had a feeling martial law was coming, and wanted to get into our RV and get the hell out. So here we are."

"We don't really have much tying us to San Diego," Linda said. "No family. The condo is on the 15th floor, so nobody is breaking in unless the whole building goes."

"So what are you going to do, go back when this all blows over?" asked Frank.

"Maybe," Hank said. "Or maybe we'll just rent it out and live in the RV full time. That pusher is big enough."

"We really weren't using that condo to its full potential anyway," Linda said. "Living right near the water seemed neat when we bought the place, but we never really did much down there. Too crowded, too expensive, too many drunks walking around. Bad traffic, bad parking. To heck with it. Maybe it would have been more fun when we were both twenty five, but who can afford such a place at that age?" She laughed heartily again. Frank and Jane joined her.

"Well, I did enjoy my telescope," Hank said, and then he laughed. Linda gave him an exasperated glance.

"Great, now these folks will think you're a pervert," she said.

"Oh, looking at some of the young lovelies on the beach, eh," said Frank. He started laughing with Hank.

"Men," Jane said, shaking her head and grinning.

"I know, huh?" Linda said with a sheepish grin.

"I think it's post time," Frank said, standing up. "Want a beer?"

"No thanks, but I'll go grab myself a glass of wine and be back in a minute," Hank said. "You want a glass, dear?"

"Sure, if our neighbors don't mind us hanging around for a little while."

"We enjoy the company," Jane said with a smile. "Honey, grab me a beer too, will you?"

"Of course," Frank said as he walked into the coach. Lucy followed him, her tail wagging.

"Oh, and why don't you feed the critters? It's about time."

"Alright," Frank said from inside.

He went to the fridge, opened it, and quickly pulled out the pet food cans and the beer. He tried to close it as fast as he could. *Conserve those batteries,* he thought to himself. Mr. Wonderful came running over when he pulled the plastic lid off the cat food.

"Well, there you are, sir," Frank said, laughing. Lucy was there too, looking up at him and wagging her tail. Frank filled their food dishes and set them down on opposite sides of the salon. Then he opened the two beers and walked outside.

"Our children are fed," Frank said, grinning. Linda gave him a quizzical look.

"He means our cat and our dog," Jane said, laughing. "Did Mr. Wonderful show up?"

"Yep, a split second after I took the lid off of the cat food can," Frank said, cracking up.

Hank came walking back over, a glass of wine in each hand.

"Here you go, baby," he said, handing a glass to Linda. He sat down.

"So, Montana, eh," Frank said. "You really think you need to go up that far?"

"That remains to be seen," Hank said. "There are some bad problems on the border, and I can see the government needing to declare martial law there. I don't trust those guys, though. I'm afraid they are going to go farther than they need to."

"Don't get wound up, Hank," Linda said.

"I've had the same kind of thoughts," Frank said. "I don't trust this Administration. In fact, I didn't trust the last Administration either, and it was the other party."

"So, if we find ourselves under martial law in the entire country, what will you do, Frank?" asked Hank.

Frank sat silently for a few seconds, looking down at his lap. Then he looked up.

"Fight."

"Oh, come on, Frank," said Jane. "This is ludicrous."

"No, I won't shut up. If this government puts the entire nation under martial law because of this border problem, we'll have to take up arms. If we don't, our liberty will be lost. I won't let that happen to my kids without a fight."

"Don't you think you are being a little paranoid?" Jane asked.

"Maybe. We'll wait and see. I just keep thinking back to Sean."

"Sean?" asked Hank.

"Sean and his wife Sarah were camped next to us at the place in Quartzsite," Frank said. "He was working as a civilian at the Marine Corps Air Station just outside of Yuma."

"You sure you want to go there, Frank?" asked Jane. "We don't know what happened."

"Yes," Frank said. "But I'll only say what we saw. They can draw their own conclusions."

Jane nodded.

"Anyway, Sean pulled me aside and started telling me things he had heard about the border problems. He said the group that just took over most of Iraq has been sending people into Mexico through Venezuela, and that they are stirring up the problems."

"Not surprising," Hank said. "I've figured something like that was going on when I saw those other folks in San Diego."

"It was worse than that. He went on to say that our government was in bed with these folks, and they were planning to use it to put the entire country under martial law. Sean said this was because putting people under tighter control was the only way to put climate change policies in place."

“Heard those rumors before myself,” said Hank. “Never put much stock in them.”

“Me neither. So anyway, we spend the night in Quartzsite. The next morning, things are starting to get a little scary there, so we get ready to take off. We were both planning to go to the same place. Flagstaff. We were going to meet up there.”

“We were planning to go through there too, originally,” Linda said. Hank nodded in agreement.

“We get on the road, fighting our way up a very crowded Route 60. Sean took off with his 5th wheel right before we left, and was far enough ahead that we couldn’t see him anymore. When we get to Route 71 the traffic thinned way down, and we were catching up to him. We could see him up ahead. Then we see two DPS cruisers and a Humvee go flying by us on the left.”

“Uh oh,” Hank said. Both he and Linda were mesmerized.

“They pull over Sean’s rig. We kept driving. Last thing I saw in my mirror were two soldiers pointing their rifles into Sean’s truck.”

“Holy crap,” Hank said. “This is bad.”

Jane shook her head.

“Frank, you and I both discussed other reasons why this might not be as ominous as you just made it sound.”

“I know,” he replied. “I’ve been thinking a lot about it since. None of those other ideas make sense to me anymore.”

“What were the other ideas, Jane,” asked Linda.

“We have some reason to believe that Sean wasn’t completely truthful with us. Of course, our first thought was that the authorities were afraid he was going to spread these stories he told us. But then we thought there were other possibilities. Maybe he was still in the service, and went AWOL. He still had the military haircut, and acted like military. Or maybe he took some things before he left the base. Or maybe he hurt somebody or did something else wrong there.”

“I’m with Frank on this one, I think,” Hank said. “There’s a real crap storm going on right now. The Marines aren’t going to be sending a Humvee with a police escort up this way for any of those things you mentioned. At least not quickly. But if things are really as he described, I could see them going after him to keep him from spilling the beans to the public.”

Frank nodded. Jane was quiet, and she looked worried. Linda looked downright scared.

"Does Sean know your last names?" asked Linda. She glanced around the camp, looking as if she expected the boogie man to rush out at her.

"No," Jane said. "They never asked. We also paid cash at that campground, and we never signed a register, so with a little luck they won't be able to find us."

"I suspect you two are boondocking because of this, though," Hank said.

"Yes," Frank said. "We've also kept our cellphones off, except for at Starbucks."

"Good call on the phones and the boondocking, but you ought to add some solar panels. I've read about these Georgetowns. Not enough battery to boondock for long with that residential fridge."

"I know," Frank said. "We were going to get solar installed in Quartzsite. Didn't seem like a good idea to stick around there, though."

"If you're going up north, you should be able to get solar installed in Kanab. Hopefully things will be alright there."

The four of them were silent for a few moments. Then they heard a gunshot coming from the motor home parked to the right. They all jerked their heads around. Another shot rang out, and then silence.

Chapter 7 - Goodnight Chief

"Hit the dirt," Frank cried, and they all got off their chairs and onto the ground. They waited. All they could hear was Lucy's frenzied barking.

"Sounded like it came from inside that other rig," Hank said. "Have you met them yet?"

"No," Frank said. "We had the clearing to ourselves when we left to go to Starbucks."

"They were already here when we pulled in," Linda said. "Can we get up now?"

"Probably," Frank said. "I think the shooting is over."

The two couples got to their feet. Several men were running over from the clearing next to theirs.

"What happened?" shouted the first man, who was wearing a hand gun in what looked like a police belt and holster. He was wearing jeans and a white T-shirt, and looked to be about forty years old, with salt and pepper hair and a big mustache.

"We don't know," Frank said. "I think the shots came from inside that motor home over there." Frank pointed it out.

"Oh, no, that's the chief's rig," said the man. He ran over to the rig, crouched, and slowly walked around the perimeter. The other men scurried over to join the first man.

"Chief, are you in there?" shouted the first man. "It's Dave. Ken and Lewis are with me."

Silence.

One of the three men came running over to Frank.

"Do you have a ladder, by any chance?" he asked.

"Yes. Won't get you on the roof, but you should be able to look in the windows," Frank said. He turned and went to the rear compartment, opening it up.

"Need a hand?" Hank asked.

"No, I'm good. It's near the top." Frank pulled it out and brought it over to one of the men, who picked it up and carried it quickly over to the rig. He placed it next to the coach door and climbed up to look through the window.

"Oh, no," he said.

"What?" the first man shouted.

"Blood all over the floor," he replied, his voice trembling.

"Try the door, Ken," said the first man.

Ken got off the ladder and set it aside. Then he pulled on the door handle. It opened, and the coach steps extended under the door.

"It was unlocked," he shouted.

The other two men came running around to the door, and they went in. Then they came back out and walked over to Frank and Jane's rig. One of the men brought the ladder with him.

"Much obliged to you," the first man said, and he leaned the ladder against the coach.

"What happened?" asked Jane. She had a worried look on her face.

"My police chief and his wife," the first man said. "Looks like a double suicide to me." He broke down crying.

"Oh no. I'm so sorry," Jane said.

"Should we call the police?" Frank asked.

"We are the police…or we were the police," the first man said. "I'm Dave."

"I'm Ken," the second man said. He was young, dressed in cargo shorts and a tank top. The black leather gun belt looked out of place with those clothes. He had dark sable brown hair that was looking a little shaggy.

"I'm Lewis," said the third man. He was in his thirties, wearing jeans and a button-down shirt. He was the tallest of the three, with light brown wavy hair.

"I'm Frank, and this is my wife Jane, and Hank and his wife Linda."

"Glad to meet you," Dave said. You guys traveling together?"

"No, we just met about half an hour ago," Hank said. "We got here a little before that. The other rig was already here."

"We were at Starbucks when it arrived," Jane said. "We only got here a couple of hours ago ourselves, so that rig couldn't have been here longer than an hour and a half."

"Thanks," Dave said.

"This doesn't surprise me," Lewis said. "The boss was pretty upset yesterday."

"What happened?" asked Frank. Lewis, Ken, and Dave looked at each other.

"Oh, what the heck, we've already dropped out," Dave said. "We all quit our job in protest."

"Why?" asked Hank.

"Feds," Dave said. He looked over at Lewis and Ken. Lewis's face was turning red, tears still streaming down his cheeks.

"Those creeps have been telling all of the local police chiefs and sheriffs in Arizona to get ready to start gun confiscations, in prep for martial law. Chief Watkins told us about it last night. He told the Feds to stick it, and said he was going to bug out."

"I knew it," Hank said, shaking his head. Ken looked over at him and shook his head in agreement.

"The chief said he hadn't found even one department that was going to comply," Ken said. "He said it was going to get rough, and that we ought to get the hell out."

"Why do you think he killed himself?" asked Linda.

"The chief was an older man," Dave said. "He was going to retire at the end of the month. His wife had Alzheimer's, and she was getting to the point that he couldn't work and take care of her."

"She's the other person in the coach?" Linda asked.

"Yes," Dave said, and he broke down again. "She was such a sweet lady." Ken and Lewis came over and put their hands on his shoulders.

"Dave, let's go get the shovels," Lewis said. "I think we'd better bury them here."

"Yeah, it's a good place. The chief loved it here," Ken said.

"Alright," Dave said. "I'll pull myself together. Sorry."

"We'd be happy to lend a hand," Frank said.

"Much obliged," said Dave, "but we'll bury our own."

Frank nodded, and the three men walked slowly back over to their camp.

The two couples looked at each other silently. Frank saw the horrified look on Jane's face. He pulled her to him and held on tight, feeling her start to sob. She pulled away so she could look at him in the face.

"I'm so sorry, Frank," she said.

"For what?"

"You know," she said.

"What, the fact that we don't agree on politics? This is not that. Differences of opinion about how to run a free society are healthy. That's not what this is. This is tyranny. The vermin that has infested our government fooled everybody, supporters and the opposition alike. This is no longer a left or right issue."

Hank and Linda watched silently. Hank pulled Linda to himself and hugged her.

Jane sat down on her chair, and Frank sat down next to her. He moved his chair closer, and put his hand on her lap. She placed her hand over his. Hank and Linda sat down too.

"So what now?" asked Linda. "Is Montana far enough?"

"We have a bigger question," Hank said. "Do we run, or do we stand and fight."

Frank looked over at Hank and nodded solemnly. Jane and Linda looked at him silently.

“I don’t think we should decide what to do next until we’ve had more conversation with Dave and his guys,” Frank said. “That can’t happen until they’ve tended to the death of their friend.”

“Agreed,” Hank said. “They know things that we’ll never hear about any other way.”

Dave, Ken, and Lewis came walking back over with shovels. They nodded as they walked by.

“I wonder how many people are in their group?” asked Jane. “Might be a good group to tag along with.”

“Maybe, if they’d let us,” Hank said.

“They might be targets, you know,” said Linda, “if they walked out of their law enforcement jobs to avoid orders from the Feds.”

“Good point,” Jane said. “Remember what happened to Sean. They might try to quiet anybody who knows anything.”

“They're also likely to be on the front lines of any battle that comes up,” Linda said.

“That’s a bad thing?” asked Hank.

Linda shook her head, looking at Hank and then Frank.

“Why don’t you two look in the mirror? Last I checked, neither of you are twenty-five. We’re too old for this sort of thing.”

"They drafted men up to age forty-five in World War II," Frank said.

"And you're about fifteen years older than that, dear," Jane said. "I understand how you feel. There are always things we can do other than fight."

"What chance do we have against the Feds, anyway?" Linda asked.

Hank laughed.

"The Feds can't win," he said. "For one thing, there are 270 million guns in the hands of private citizens in this country, and that's not counting the millions of guns that have been purchased before we had mandatory registration. But that's not the only problem the Feds have. Half of their forces would desert before helping them take over. They obviously can't count on local law enforcement either. Look at our friends burying their dead right now. The Feds think they can count on these folks. I doubt it."

"That's a really good point," Frank said. He looked at Jane. "Remember that CHP officer that talked to us at the check point? He said 'Do you have any guns? *Say no*' – remember?"

"Yes, I remember," Jane said. "You have to be careful drawing conclusions off such a small sample size, though."

"True enough," Hank said. "What check point?"

"It was a ways past where our RV Storage lot was, on I-10."

"We saw a kid get shot there," Jane said. "It was horrible."

"It was a gang member, but he couldn't have been more than sixteen years old," Frank said. "He was running away, shooting at the CHP officers. Two soldiers opened fire on him."

"Wow," Linda said. "Glad we got out of California before things got that bad."

"Seriously," Hank said.

"I can't tell how worried Dave and his friends are," Frank said. "For all we know, they have guards posted at their campground."

"Possible," Hank said. "I think we'd better go get our firearms into a place where we can get at them. Let's go back to the coach for a while, Linda."

The two got up.

"Thanks so much for the company," Linda said. "We'll talk to you later."

"Alright, sounds like a plan," Frank said. He got up and shook hands with Hank.

"Bye now," Jane said.

Frank sat back down by Jane and watched them walk away. They could hear the shovels digging into the soft soil under the pine trees, about forty yards away. There was no conversation coming from there.

"I think we should get our guns out into a place where we can get at them too," Frank said. He got up and started towards the door of their coach.

"Wait for me," Jane said, and she rushed to follow him.

They both climbed into the coach. Frank unhooked the front bunk and pulled it free, then unfolded it. He carefully removed the guns and the ammo, and put them in front of the couch. Then he closed the front bunk again. Mr. Wonderful sauntered out to him and rubbed against his leg.

"Well, look who's here," Frank said. He squatted down to pet the cats head.

"He likes that," Jane said. I'm surprised the gunshots didn't spook him."

"Speaking of that, where's Lucy?"

"Good question. I'll go check in the bedroom."

Lucy was sitting just inside the bedroom. She looked up at Jane as she walked back, and her tail began wagging. She nuzzled Jane's leg as she sat down on the bed.

"You alright, girl?" Jane asked. "Come on up."

Lucy jumped up onto the bed and got on Jane's lap.

"Uh oh, cleanup on aisle three," Jane said.

"What?" Frank asked, walking towards the bedroom.

"Our girl had an accident. Watch your step."

"Oh, poor thing," Frank said. He went back to the kitchen sink and pulled several paper towels off of the roll. He cleaned up the mess. "It's okay, girl."

"Frank, what are we going to do? And what about Robbie? We can't even get to him to help him now. What if he gets into trouble?"

"Let's just take it slow and think carefully." We might want to head up to Oregon and get Sarah. That's liable to follow California."

"I know, I was thinking that," Jane said. "We need to get a message off to her next time we get a chance."

Frank nodded, and then got up and went out into the salon. He picked up the shot gun and put it between the wall and the driver's seat, with one of the boxes of shells. He leaned the rifle up in the hallway just before the bedroom, out of site from the front, but easy to get to. The ammo for that went into the pantry next to where it leaned. Then he carried the pistol into the bedroom and put it under his pillow.

"Maybe you should wear that pistol," Jane said.

"I haven't dug the holster out of the back compartment yet," Frank said. "And it's too bulky to wear anyway."

"Where's the ammo?"

"It's the same kind as the Winchester lever gun uses.

"Shit, you brought the .44 mag? Why'd you bring one that I can't shoot?"

"I had a lot of ammo for that. We've got about four hundred rounds. Most of it is out next to the tools in the right storage compartment. If you need to shoot, either the Winchester or the shotgun would be better anyway. You never practiced much with pistols."

"Okay, makes sense. Now I wish we would have brought more of the guns."

"I didn't think we'd get these out of California."

Jane nodded. "Hungry?"

"I could eat a little something, but a Clif Bar would be enough for now."

"Okay. We should eat some of the bananas too. They were a few days old when we left."

"Good." Frank went out and sat in the dinette, watching Dave and his men out the window. He saw them carry an old woman's body out and drop it into a hole.

Jane sat down next to Frank and handed him a banana and a bar. Then she looked out the window.

"Looks like they are getting close to done."

"Yep," Frank said. "I'm going to go sit outside when they are finished and try to get their attention for a moment. I want to ask them if it's safe to be here."

"Okay, I'll go out there with you."

They finished their snacks in silence. They were both exhausted.

"We'd better get out there, looks like they're done," Jane said. Frank nodded, and they both got up and went out the door, leaving Lucy inside.

"Here they come," Jane said as she sat down. Frank walked out to meet them.

"Can I ask you guys a few questions?"

Dave smiled at him and they stopped.

"Of course," he said.

"Is it safe to be here?"

"It's not safe to be anywhere," Dave said. "We're going to make it a little safer here though. We're going to drive the Chief's rig back up 4th Street a ways, and then off on a long dirt road to the right."

"That's going to make us safer?"

"Yep, because when I get there, I'm going to turn on all of the chief's electronics, and then I'm going to place a call to the police station. I know those creeps are monitoring that."

Frank grinned. "Good idea."

"You folks know to keep your phones off, right?" asked Ken.

"Yes, the only time we turned them on was when we went to Starbucks earlier today. I doubt they are looking for us, though. We don't know anything."

"We don't know for sure what they're doing at this point," Dave said. "I've heard some people saying that the Feds are looking into anybody that has a cellular or GPS hit away from their home address."

"Geez," Frank said.

"I still think we ought to set up a booby trap in the Chief's RV," Ken said.

"Love to do that, son," Dave said, "but they would figure out who did it, and then they would be hunting us big time. Besides, we might take out somebody who is really on our side. I don't want to take that risk."

“Simmons is out looking for us now, I suspect,” Lewis said. “Luckily that idiot can’t find his ass with both hands.”

“Who’s Simmons?” Frank asked.

“Officer Simmons. One of two officers that decided to stay on the job after the Chief told us what was going on. He’s a real Nazi. Was kicked out of two metro departments for bad conduct.”

“This isn’t that far from town,” Frank said. “Why can’t he find you?”

“He’s only been here a few months, and he hates camping. He doesn’t know about this place. But if he does figure out where we are, he won’t be around long enough to tell anybody.”

“So you guys are going to stick around here for now?”

“Yes, but if I were you folks, I wouldn’t,” Dave said.

“Understand. We were planning to go north another state or two.”

“I’d make it three,” Lewis said. “We best be going, Dave, if we are going to get the Chief’s rig out of here tonight.”

Dave nodded, and the three men continued back to their camp.

Frank walked back over to the chairs and sat down next to Jane.

"Well?" she asked.

"Dave suggested that we not stick around here very long. He says go two or three states to the north."

"What are they going to do?"

"Stay and fight."

"Oh." Jane had a worried look on her face. "You *are* okay with going, right?"

"I want to see if we can get to our daughter," Frank said. "That's north."

"What else did they say?"

"They said to leave cellphones off, because rumor has it that the Feds are matching cellular and GPS hits to people's home addresses. If you aren't at home, you might get a visit."

"Glad we have kept ours off. What else?"

"They're going to drive the Chief's rig back down 4th street, and then off in another direction, down a really long dirt road. Then they're going to turn on the Chief's cellphone and make a call with it to the police station."

Jane got a grin on her face.

"Wild goose chase, eh," she said.

"Yep. And if we get stopped by an Officer Simmons when we're around here, don't trust him."

"Why?"

“He's good with what the Feds asked the department to do, and he has a very questionable past.”

“Wonderful,” Jane said. Then she heard something. A helicopter, sounding too low, coming towards them. They saw it after a few seconds.

“Shit!” Frank said. “That isn’t one of ours. It’s Russian made. Let’s get into the trees.”

They both got up. Jane opened the door and grabbed Lucy, and they ran for the trees.

Chapter 8 - Air Assault

Frank and Jane cowered under the trees, watching the helicopter as it took a long slow look at their area. Hank and Linda came running over, crouching. They stood up when they got under the trees.

"That looks like a Russian chopper," Frank said.

"You're right, that's a Mil Mi-24 variant, one of their export models."

"You know something about these?" asked Frank.

"Yeah, part of my training back in my Air National Guard days."

"Any chance it belongs to Venezuela?"

Hank looked over at Frank, and nodded yes.

"Hey, there's another one!" Jane said, pointing.

Hank looked up, and got a shocked look on his face.

"What the heck. That's an Apache. It's one of ours. Why doesn't he attack?"

"Looks to me like they're working together, looking for something," Frank said.

"Yes, it does," Hank said. "This is a little disturbing."

"Maybe they're looking for the Chief's coach," Linda said.

"It might be too far under the trees to see," Frank said.

"Oh, crap, see the way the Mi-24 is angling? It's getting ready to fire," Hank said.

Fire shot out of the front of the gun, and then there was a loud explosion, over about two clearings. Smoke billowed up.

"Maybe we'd better get further into the woods," Jane said.

"Yes, I think you're right," Hank said. They started back in when they heard the sound of a jet. Suddenly both helicopters exploded, pieces flying in every direction. Hank ran out into the clearing just in time to see an F-16 fly over and climb, turning around to go back towards the east.

"Yahooooo!" shouted Hank.

The others ran out to join him, watching the debris fall.

"Who was that?" Frank asked.

"Texas Air National Guard, baby!" he replied. "I'd know that insignia anywhere."

"Texans shooting down an Apache?" Jane asked. "Does that seem right to you?"

"Let's think this through," Frank said. "Two possibilities. The Apache could have been captured by the enemy in this border war, or elements of the Federal Government are working with the enemy, making the border war a false flag attack."

"I'd say your second scenario is more likely," Hank said. "Those choppers knew that there were possibly resistance fighters in these woods. Foreign enemies of the US wouldn't have that information, and more importantly, they wouldn't care. These woods have no strategic value. Either does this piss-ant road to nowhere."

"True," Frank said. "If they were just the enemy, they would have gone up north a few miles and blown up I-40, since that's a good way to get military supplies from the interior of the country to the battle zone."

"Exactly," Hank replied.

"Listen to yourselves," Jane said. "Seriously? You really think the US Government would team up with foreign fighters to start up a civil war?"

"Well, bringing foreigners in for a situation like this is not unusual," Hank said. "The confederacy tried to do exactly that with England during our first civil war."

"First civil war," Linda said. She was on the verge of tears. Hank saw that, and pulled her close.

Frank saw movement out of the corner of his eye. It was Dave, Ken, and Lewis, trotting over to them.

"You folks alright?" asked Dave, out of breath.

"Yes, we're all good," Frank said. "Just a little shook up. You?"

"They hit our decoy campground. These people are stupid," Lewis said.

"Decoy campground?" asked Frank.

"Yeah," Ken said. "These guys laughed at me when I got the idea. We took off with the police department's paddy wagon. I parked it way back there, and I set a bunch of pup tents around it, in the open. It's in a clearing about 500 yards that way." He pointed.

Hank cracked up. "Seriously?"

Dave got an embarrassed smile on his face, and nodded.

"I didn't think it would work," he said. "Never underestimate the kids."

"I'd better get going with the Chief's rig," Lewis said. He went over to the coach and opened the door. "Ken, you're going to follow me in your jeep, right?"

"Yeah, I'll be behind you. Wish we had more pup tents."

Lewis shook his head with a grin, and closed the coach door. Then the engine fired up, and the coach slowly lumbered towards the dirt road.

"I'd best be going," Ken said.

"Be careful," Dave said. "If you hear any aircraft, get under the trees fast."

"Gotcha, boss," Ken said.

"Don't call me boss," Dave said. Ken nodded and waved as he trotted back to their camp.

"We were lucky," Dave said. "If they would have come earlier in the day, they would have seen reflections of our rigs under those trees."

"I'm sure they saw our rigs," Hank said.

"They didn't match the description that Officer Simmons provided, I would imagine. Luckily there are a lot of folks camped around here."

"They're coming back, aren't they?" asked Linda.

"Almost certainly," Dave said. "The Texicans will be back too. I have a connection there. I tipped them off to keep an eye out, but I probably didn't need to. They have a good view of the whole southwest. They probably saw those choppers coming this way from Yuma, or even Southern California."

"So Texas is fighting the Federal Government?" asked Jane.

"Among other states," Dave said. "The Feds think they have Arizona under control." He got a sly grin on his face.

"This is crazy," Jane said. "Why isn't there coverage of this on the media?"

Dave just looked at her, as if she was telling him she just saw a unicorn.

"I knew something was wrong before we left San Diego," Hank said. "Like I was telling these folks, I started to see a lot of immigrants that didn't look Hispanic to me. They were speaking in Arabic."

"You guys got out of California?" asked Dave. "You're lucky."

"We left San Diego about a week ago," Linda said.

"You have family there?" asked Dave.

"No," Linda replied. "But Frank and Jane have a son where they're from."

"Where is that?"

"Redondo Beach," Frank said. "Up the coast about two hours from San Diego."

"I know where that is. Nice area," Dave said. "Your son is probably safer in Redondo Beach than he would be in San Diego. San Diego is a Fed staging point now, but there are a lot of rednecks in the area between San Diego and LA. Believe it or not, the gangs in the LA area are now openly fighting the military, side by side with middle class white folks."

"You're kidding," Jane said. "The gang activity is what forced us out of there."

"Yup, they were having a real free for all before they realized what the Feds were up to."

Linda looked like she was about to double over. She was trembling.

"Are you having a panic attack, honey?" asked Hank.

She nodded, and Hank walked her back over to their RV.

"It's going to get worse before it gets better," Dave said. "Commerce is shutting down in a lot of areas, especially in California. Most people don't realize how much of our food comes from there."

"How are you getting all this news?" asked Jane.

"Other police organizations," Dave said. "And the internet."

"Can you trust the internet?" Jane asked. "Lots of nut balls on there."

"The internet is going to be the undoing of the Feds," Dave said.

"He's right, honey," Frank said. "It was designed with so much redundancy that it's nearly impossible to shut down. Add to that the fact that very few of the brightest internet folks are working for the Feds."

"The internet is being used to send the real news out, and to coordinate the resistance," Dave said.

"Maybe this is how you can get involved, honey," Jane said. Frank nodded.

"What's your background, Frank?" asked Dave.

"I ran network security for one of the largest aerospace companies before I retired."

"How long ago did you retire?"

"Only six months ago, so I'm still up on the latest," Frank said.

"I know some people you could talk to," Dave said. "I won't lie to you, though. All of those folks have a big target on their backs."

"Not surprising, but I don't care," Frank said. "I've had a good long life in this country, and I'll be damned if I'm going to sit back and watch her go down the tubes. I've got my kids to think about, and our future generations."

Hank came walking back over.

"How is she?" asked Jane.

"She took her meds, so she'll sleep for a while. This is a lot to take in."

"I'll say," Jane replied.

"What'd I miss?"

"We were talking about the internet," Frank said. "Sounds like I might be of some value."

"Really," Hank said. "Internet was my day job too. E-commerce. What did you do?"

"Network security at one of the big Aerospace companies."

"Really," Hank said. "If you don't mind me asking, what's your last name?"

"Johnson."

Hank's face lit up.

"I know who you are. I've read some of your white papers."

Dave got a quizzical look on his face. Hank saw that.

"This guy has published a lot of cutting edge technical articles about networks and the internet," Hank said. "Some people think he's a genius."

"Oh, please," Frank said. Jane laughed.

"Were you really going to stay retired?" Hank asked.

"Yes," Frank replied. "I got tired of trying to convince executives that their intellectual property was in danger. And people wonder how China is developing their military hardware so quickly. Idiots."

"Well, I'd better get back," Dave said. "Feel free to come over to our camp if you need anything. And I'll pass your name along to my sources."

"Alright, see you later," Hank said. Frank and Jane both nodded, and Dave walked away.

"So what else did I miss?" asked Hank.

"Dave had quite a bit of info, actually," Jane said. "You heard when he said that San Diego is now a staging point for the Feds, but the area between San Diego and LA is not yet under control."

"Yeah, Dave said that the gangs in LA are now fighting the US military, side by side with middle class white folk," Frank said. "And that's how we got on the internet, right?"

"That's right," Jane said. "He said that the internet was being used for news and for coordination of the resistance."

"Then it's true," Hank said.

"What's true?" asked Jane.

"Rumors I've been seeing on the internet, on discussion threads," Hank said. "The American people are figuring out what is going on very quickly, and the Feds didn't count on that. They were hoping that they could get us fighting each other in a civil war. That's not going to end well for them."

“Why would the Federal Government want to get a civil war started?” asked Jane. “This just sounds like more paranoid far-right garbage to me.”

“A controlled civil war would kill off a lot of people the Feds consider ‘undesirables’,” Hank said, “and would allow them to swoop in and stop the fighting at a time of their choosing. Then they'd reform the government with certain changes. You know, like no more Bill of Rights. They would be free to mold us into the great utopia that they haven’t been able to sell to us any other way.”

Jane looked over at Frank. He was deep in thought.

“So you're basically saying that the Federal Government is completely evil, and would allow the killing of millions in order to put the American people under control. Is that it?” Jane asked. Her face was turning a red and her eyes were getting glassy.

“Calm down, honey,” Frank said.

“Aren’t you going to say anything? She asked. He just nodded no.

“Why did an Apache helicopter and a foreign Mi-24 work together to fire at the decoy campsite?” asked Hank.

“I don’t know,” Jane said. She looked silently down at the ground for a moment.

Then she looked back up at Hank. "You haven't been saying this sort of thing in front of Linda."

"Linda has really bad anxiety problems. It was hard to get her to leave our condo, although I know she's glad now that we did. I've kept track of what is going on as much as I can, but I haven't been saying anything to her about it."

"Probably a good idea, given her problems," Frank said. "This is hard to fathom for anybody. Just weeks ago we thought we were about to embark on our golden years, happily traveling around a peaceful countryside in our motor home. That's all gone now."

Jane looked down, and started sobbing again. Frank went over and put his arms around her.

"I'm sorry honey," he said.

"They're going to beat us," Jane said. "A few renegade states don't have the resources to beat the Federal armed forces. They control everything."

"That's where you're wrong, Jane," Hank said. "I know why the gangs and the middle-class folks are fighting together."

"Why?" Frank asked, still holding onto Jane.

"Escondido."

"What about it?"

"I saw some reports and YouTube videos coming out over the last few days. It's gone viral. The Feds are really stupid."

Jane broke the hug, getting herself together again. She looked over at Hank.

"So what happened there, Hank?" she asked.

"The Feds thought they could control these jihadist idiots from Iraq, just like they thought they could control the Muslim Brotherhood and the Mujahideen. Wrong."

"Uh oh," Frank said.

"Yeah, uh oh," Hank said. "Some jihadists go into Escondido and decide it is a good city to try out the old 'convert or die' routine. Bad idea. There's a lot of rednecks in Escondido."

"Go on," Frank said.

"The jihadists started executing people who resisted them in public. Beheadings and hangings. Real nasty stuff. That was along with the general terror these thugs do in their own countries - things such as raping teenage girls and boys."

"Sick," Jane said.

"A lot of this stuff got out on the internet, on YouTube and other sites. It went viral in a matter of hours. Then the citizens of

Escondido got together and ambushed these creeps. Killed them all."

"Geez," Jane said.

"It gets worse. They dug a big pit, and they tossed the bodies of the dead jihadists in. Then they dumped all kinds of pig blood on top, and covered it up with dirt. And of course there was video taken of the whole thing, and it all got out onto the internet. The next day thousands of jihadists arrived, and started killing everybody they could find."

"What did they expect?" Jane said.

"You haven't heard the best part yet. The citizens were holding them off, and starting to win the battle. Never underestimate rednecks with guns. Then the US army came in and helped the jihadists. That also was captured quite well on video and sent out on the internet. What do you think the public's reaction was to that?"

"Oh, I don't know, perhaps gang members and middle class folks getting together to attack the army," Frank said. "The Feds just lost this war. They would need an army of millions to defeat the people of this country."

"Exactly, but it's still going to be a very bloody affair, and it's going to go on for a while. The cat is most definitely out of the bag, though. No putting it back. The citizens are on to them."

"You two look like you're happy about this," Jane said.

"Well, I am," Hank said. "The jihadists were going to do this either way. They chose to do it sooner rather than later - and didn't give the Feds enough time to get the American people fighting each other. Now the Feds will never be able to do that."

"The Feds would have lost anyway," Frank said. "Eventually, at least."

"I know, but this will be less costly to the people."

Jane shook her head.

"I'm still not completely buying all of this," she said.

"Look, here comes Dave," Frank said. He was trotting over.

"Pack up, folks, we got to leave in a hurry."

"Why," asked Jane.

"Ground troops are on the way here. I just got tipped off. They are about half an hour away. They plan on scouring this whole area."

"Where to?" Hank asked.

"Go back through Williams, and go north on Route 64," Dave said.

Frank and Jane looked at each other, and bolted for their rig.

"I'll get the rig pulled forward enough to get the Jeep attached. You pull in behind me and we'll get it hooked up."

Hank trotted over to his rig, with Dave next to him.

"So Dave, what's going to keep us from being blown off the highway?"

"We'll have some air support," Dave said, grinning. He kept running after Hank arrived at his coach.

It took Frank and Jane only a few minutes to get the Jeep hooked up. Frank looked over and saw that Hank was about ready to leave too. Jane waved at him as they pulled onto the dirt road.

"Wait a minute, I'm going to bring the pistol up here," Frank said. He ran to the bedroom, grabbed the large revolver, and picked up a box of ammo on the way up. He put the revolver in his lap and the box of shells on the floor between the driver's seat and the wall. He checked the pistol to make sure it was loaded. Then he drove out onto the dirt road.

"Geez, I'm glad we got some warning," Jane said.

"You and me both," Frank said. Lucy came running up to the front and jumped on Jane's lap.

"I can see three rigs behind us," Frank said. They were nearing 4th street. Then they saw it. A police vehicle was parked across the dirt road. A tall lanky officer was leaned up against his car, holding a shotgun.

"Oh no," Jane said.

Frank slowed down and stopped. The officer smiled, and walked over to the window. Frank opened it.

"Where are you nice folks going," asked the officer. Frank looked down at him. His name tag said 'Simmons'.

Chapter 9 - News from Home

Officer Simmons craned his neck to get a look into the coach. Frank could feel his hand sweating around the grip of the big .44 magnum pistol. Lucy was growling. Jane tried to calm her down.

"I asked where you folks were going," Simmons said with an impatient tone of voice.

"North, sir," Frank said. His voice trembled.

"Come out of the coach. I need to search for weapons. If I find any, you'll be held until Federal forces arrive."

"Why?"

"Don't ask me any questions, just follow instructions," he spat, his hand moving on the shotgun.

"No," Frank said. Then he pulled the trigger on the big .44, sending the officer flying backwards. The shotgun flew out of his hands and landed in the bushes.

"Frank!" shouted Jane, horrified. "What did you do?"

Frank was trembling hard. He saw Dave running over in his side mirror.

"Frank, you alright?" shouted Dave.

"Yes, but there's a shotgun down there somewhere, and I don't think I killed this guy."

Ken came running up behind Dave.

"Thanks a lot, Frank, I wanted to shoot this jerk weed," he said.

"He's still alive, barely," said Dave, kneeling by him. Ken picked up the shotgun out of a ditch by the road, and Dave pulled the pistol out of Simmons's holster. Then he grabbed the keys off Simmons's belt and tossed them to Ken. Ken nodded at him, and got into the police car. He fired it up and moved it away from the road.

"Sorry you had to go through this, folks," Dave said.

"Is he still alive?" asked Jane.

"Unfortunately, yes," Dave said. "What kind of pistol do you have, Frank? It blew a good-sized hole through your rig."

"I've got an old Ruger Blackhawk .44 mag," Frank said. He held it up.

"That thing saved your life. Probably all of our lives. He would have shot you two and made sure none of the rest of us could get past your rig."

Ken came running back over.

"We'd better get out of here, boss. The clock is running. We don't want to be here when the army shows up."

"Yeah, let's get moving," Dave said. "And quit calling me boss."

"What about the traitor?"

"We've got his guns. I'll put a couple rounds in his tires on the way out. His pelvis is pretty screwed up, so he isn't going to get up and walk. I say we just leave him in the ditch."

Ken nodded.

"Alright, Frank, let's get moving," Dave said. "Don't stop for anything. Get up to Route 64, and follow that to Route 89 north."

"Ok," Frank said.

"And keep that pistol handy," Ken said.

Frank put the coach in gear and pulled out onto the pavement of 4th street. Then he sped up. He could see the other coaches pulling out behind him. He heard two gunshots. He kept driving.

"You alright?" he asked.

Jane looked over at him, crying.

"No, I'm not alright," she said.

"Do you think I did the wrong thing?"

"I don't know."

Frank checked his rear-view mirrors again. There were a lot of coaches behind them.

"I think every one of the rigs in that campsite are following us," Frank said.

"Do you think the army would have shot all of us?"

"I think we would have been either shot or locked up."

"I keep hearing all of you guys talking about the Federal Government, but how do you know what they're really doing? Everything we've been told so far has either been hearsay or our assumptions about things we've seen."

"The checkpoint. The helicopters."

"Yes, things look bad, but it might not be as it seems," Jane said. "And now it's going to be really hard to tell what the truth is."

"Why?" asked Frank.

"You just shot a cop. The authorities are going to be after us now even if they haven't gone bad."

Frank was starting to get angry now.

"Think about what you're saying, Jane. What right does the police have to bottle up the exit to a camping area like that? What right do they have to search without probable cause? And by the way, it's legal to have firearms in your vehicle."

"The government took firearms away from people during Katrina."

“Yes, they did, and it was wrong. Any Federal or State officials that took a part in that ought to be in jail.”

“It was a public safety issue, Frank.”

“Public safety doesn’t trump the Bill of Rights. Sorry.”

“Shut up for a minute, Frank. Listen.”

It was the sound of helicopters.

“Oh, crap, here it comes,” Frank said. “I can’t see anything in these damn mirrors.”

“I’ll go in the bedroom and check out the back window.” Jane got out of her seat, and put Lucy in her bed. She walked carefully back and raised the blinds on the back window. She could see eight helicopters flying in formation up towards the front of the line of coaches.

“See anything?” shouted Frank.

“About eight helicopters. Looks like some of them are those Russian kind, and some are the American kind. They’re going to try to get to the front of the line.”

“Shit,” Frank said. Then he saw one of the choppers in front of him. It stayed there, and then a loudspeaker came on.

“Stop your vehicle or be fired upon,” said the voice coming from the chopper. It was a Mi-24. The voice had a heavy Spanish accent.

"I'm not stopping," Frank said. "No way in hell." He sped up.

"This is your final warning," said the loudspeaker. Then they heard a different sound.

"Frank, here come the jets again. They're coming up behind us low and fast."

"Hope they're the good guys," Frank shouted.

Then there was an explosion behind them. Then another. The chopper in front of the coach made a quick turn off to the left, and was trying to get away.

"The jets shot down two of the helicopters, Frank, and the others are high-tailing it. The jets are coming around for another attack."

"Yeah, the one in front of us is heading for the hills," Frank said. His heart was beating a mile a minute.

There were two more explosions, and then another two.

"Those helicopters are no match for the jets," Jane shouted. "They're firing missiles at them two at a time."

"How many jets?"

"Hard to tell, because they come and go so fast. At least three."

Another explosion.

"Wow, only one left," Jane shouted.

“I can see that one. It’s the one that was in front of us. He’s trying to get behind the hills over there.”

The last chopper exploded while Frank was watching. Then he saw the three jets fly by, rocking their wings.

“Those jets aren’t done yet,” Jane shouted. “They are heading back towards the campground. I’m seeing puffs of smoke in the air above where we were.”

“Anti-aircraft shells, probably. The army must have gotten there.”

“Wow. Huge explosion, and fire everywhere back there,” Jane shouted. “Another explosion.”

“Can’t hear them up here,” Frank shouted.

“One of the jets just made a low pass, and a bunch of fire flowed out of the bottom.”

“Holy shit, they’re using Napalm.”

Jane got back up to the front and sat down in the passenger seat. Lucy jumped back on her lap. She was trembling as she nuzzled against Jane, and looked up at her face.

“It’s okay, girl,” said Jane, her voice wavering. She petted Lucy and looked over at Frank.

“You alright, honey?” Frank asked.

“Yes,” she said. “I’m sorry.”

“Me too.”

“We’re almost to Williams,” Frank said. “Wonder if I should take I-40 to Route 64, or take city streets?”

Suddenly a Jeep Wrangler pulled up in front of him. It was Lewis and Ken; the top was down, and Frank could see them. Lewis turned around from the passenger seat, and pointed to the I-40 east bound onramp, and then they drove in that direction. Frank followed.

“Well, that answers your question,” Jane said. “Didn’t we need some gas?”

“We’re fine. We’ve got over three quarters of a tank. I was worried about it earlier because I thought we would be boondocking for a while back there, and running the generator a lot.”

“Oh. Good.”

Frank merged onto I-40. The road was nearly empty. He sped up, trying to keep up with the jeep in front of him.

“Lucy is still pretty shook up,” Jane said, petting her on the back and trying to calm her.

“She doesn’t like the noise. She can also tell when we’re scared.”

“Yes, dogs are pretty well wired to humans,” Jane said. “It’s okay, girl.”

“We’re coming up to the turnoff to Route 64,” Frank said. “Wonder how long we'll be driving tonight? It's getting late. We'll lose sunlight before too long."

"There are quite a few campgrounds on this road," Jane said. "We're getting close to the Grand Canyon now."

"Wonder how much we'll have to slow down once we get on Route 64?"

"Good question. There it is, Frank," Jane said, pointing. The Jeep Wrangler took the off-ramp, and Frank followed, along with the other coaches. At the bottom of the ramp, they took a left turn onto Route 64.

"Well, this doesn't look too bad," Frank said. Soon they were up to about 55 mph. The road was long and straight, and the trees were gone now, giving way to small bushes and flat desert.

"This makes me nervous," Jane said. "There aren't any trees to hide behind."

"Yeah, you do feel a little exposed out here," Frank said. "And it's almost dusk. I hope Dave and his crew have a good place to stop before it gets too late."

They were quiet for a while, each thinking of all that had happened. Jane looked like she was on the verge of tears again. Frank gripped the steering wheel tightly, going over the day's events in his mind. He kept coming back to the look on Officer Simmons's face when he was shot. *I shot a police officer,* he thought to himself. *Life will never be the same.*

It finally got dark, and Frank put on his headlights. He saw the headlights of the other coaches going on in his mirror.

"Look, Frank, there's a town up there."

"Probably Valle. I saw it on the map this morning. It is the only town around for quite a ways."

"The sign says *Bedrock City*. Look," Jane said.

"There's an airfield over to the left. Ken and Lewis are pulling in over there."

The Jeep pulled over to a large flat area just on the other side of the airfield, and motioned for Frank to pull over there. Then the other coaches followed, lining up in a large row. Jane counted 23.

"Wow, there's more than I thought. Wonder how many were at the campground, and how many joined us along the way?"

"Don't know," Frank said. He shut off the engine, and got out of his seat. He stuffed the pistol in his belt. "Let's go see what's up."

"I'll take Lucy out, she's got to need it by now," Jane said. She put the leash on Lucy and headed towards the door behind Frank. As Frank opened the door, they could hear the sound of a jet coming in. He saw one land on the runway ahead of them, then another, then a third. He put his hands over his ears. Lucy barked.

After the noise died down, Frank got out, and helped Jane. She had a worried look on her face. Ken and Lewis came walking over.

"Is that who I think it is?" asked Frank. Dave walked up as he was talking.

"Yup," Dave said. "The Texans have assets positioned in several places to the east. This is one of the smaller bases. There's only the three planes here, plus support vehicles, personnel, and armaments. There are others further east, and north."

"Why doesn't the US Air force take these out?" asked Frank. "They look like sitting ducks to me."

"The US Air Force is grounded," Dave said. "The high command refused to attack civilians. They took over all of the Air Force bases. They're watching, to make sure no other country takes advantage and attacks us. Oh, and they pretty much destroyed Venezuela."

"What about those helicopters?"

"Part of the army is still serving the Feds, and they have some of the choppers. The rest belong to the invaders from south of the border. We still have drones to worry about, although the Air Force took out a lot of command and control for those."

"Cruise missiles?"

"I don't know the status of the Navy at this point, but I suspect they aren't playing ball with the Feds, or else we'd be seeing Tomahawk Missile attacks. The Air Force has the other cruise missiles."

Hank walked over.

"Hi, guys, what's up?" he asked.

"I think we should camp out here tonight, and then head north in the morning," Dave said. "Thoughts?"

"Well, I'm for it," Jane said, walking up with Lucy on the leash. "I think we're all worn out. Is it safe enough?"

"Should be, as long as no drones get through," Dave said. "And even if they did, we wouldn't be the main target. They'd go after the planes and support vehicles first."

"Can we shoot down the drones if they show up?" asked Hank.

"Possibly," Dave said. "If our planes were in the air, we could, but they aren't in the air all the time."

"Can we go talk to the pilots? Maybe they know some things that we haven't heard," Jane said.

Dave got a funny look on his face.

"We aren't allowed on that airfield," Dave said. "This is about as close as they will let us get."

Jane looked into his eyes. Something wasn't right.

"Frank, let's go inside and eat, and then get to sleep," Jane said. "I'm tired. We've been going all day."

"Alright, honey," Frank said. They got back into their coach.

"Feed the animals while I get some dinner going?" asked Jane.

"Sure." Frank got the cat and dog food out of the fridge and started filling the pet dishes. Mr. Wonderful sauntered out and rubbed against the back of Frank's legs. "Well, look who showed up."

"I can't believe that cat. Nothing scares him."

"Seriously," Frank said. "He's probably too dumb to know he should be scared." He laughed.

"Now be nice," Jane said. She was heating up some canned chili on the stove.

"That smells good, Jane. I'll get out the hot sauce."

Frank put the cat food and dog food down on the floor. Both animals came running, and started eating. Jane brought two bowls of chili and a bag of rolls over to the dinette. Frank grabbed some spoons and napkins. They both sat down to eat.

"Frank, we need to talk. And you need to have an open mind. Can you?"

Frank sighed. "Alright, tell me what's on your mind."

"I was going through the things that have happened, trying to piece together where we've gotten the info that points to this Federal takeover story. Frank, it's all hearsay from people we don't know at all. Every bit of it."

"I'm listening."

"We get comments from Sean about the Feds being in league with radical Muslims. He gets picked up on the road, and we jump to the conclusion that his story is correct."

"Alright."

"Then we meet up with Hank. He tells us a bunch of stuff about San Diego that could be true if the Feds are doing a false flag attack or not."

"Go on."

"Then there's Dave. He's telling us a lot of stuff too, none of which we can verify. It's very possible that the Texas Air National

Guard is helping the Feds to keep the bad guys from coming up the eastern flank."

Frank was silent for a moment, thinking.

"Alright, Jane, you've got my attention. And frankly, I didn't like the response Dave gave when you suggested we talk to the folks at the airfield."

"Exactly. You know what I want to ask them, correct?"

"Well, if it were me, I'd ask them if they are fighting the Federal Government."

"I think we should risk using the cellphone to call Robbie," Jane said. "I'd like to know if he's heard anything about middle class folks teaming up with the gangs to fight the Feds."

"Agreed. Call him."

"OK, I'm turning on my iPhone. Hopefully there's some cell towers around here."

"Alright. You done eating?"

"Yes, Frank, thanks," Jane said as Frank picked up the spoons and bowls and put them on the counter.

"You going to lower the jacks and put out the slides?"

"No, if you don't mind. I want to be able to get out of here in a hurry. I'm going to leave the Jeep hooked up too. We can pull straight out of here if we need to."

“No problem. Oh, the phone is ready. We have bars. I’ll call.” She dialed up the phone, and listened to it ringing.

“Mom?” asked Robbie.

“Hi, son. How are you doing?”

“Good. How are you guys? Hope you aren’t in southern Arizona.”

“No, we’re up in the middle part of that state, but heading further north soon. How are things there?”

“Quite a bit better, actually. The Martial Law is working. The looting is just about stopped here. I can’t believe how fast they were able to lock things down.”

“Really? That’s great!”

“Yeah, they divided the area into grids. You have to go through check points now, and if you can’t prove that you either live in an area or have business there, they won’t let you through. A lot of people protested, but that got over quick.”

“How big are the areas?”

“Well, your condo is close to one of the borders. It runs along Inglewood Ave, and north to Imperial Hwy. If you are east of Inglewood or north of Imperial, you can’t get in without a reason. That cut out virtually all of the troublemakers.”

"Have you heard anything about middle class folks and gangs getting together to fight the Feds?"

"That's a phony story that popped up yesterday," Robbie said. "It's all over the internet, but only on the nutcase sites. You know, the truther sites, the militia sites, and the prepper sites. At first some of the more legit outlets picked up the stories because nobody knew what was going on. They retracted them this morning."

"So it's safe there?"

"I think so, but you guys shouldn't come back yet, because there's a big mess to the south and to the east. It would be dangerous to get through all of that."

"Are you still at the condo?"

"Yes. My building got burned down. Hope you don't mind."

"You stay there as long as you want, Robbie. Here, I'll let you say hello to dad."

Jane handed the phone to Frank.

"Hi, son, how are you?"

"Doing good, dad, how are you?"

"Alright. Pretty wild times here. We drove through an air battle to get here."

"Really? You guys need to get north. There's a lot of fighting going on in southern Arizona."

"Have you heard anything about the enemy capturing US helicopters?"

"Yes, they overran a base right outside of Yuma, and got their hands on some Apache attack helicopters. We got the base back, but they still have some of the choppers. Apparently the base got infiltrated by some nutcase militia group. That's the only reason the enemy was able to take it over."

"Where did you hear this?" Frank asked.

"It's all over the cable news…CNN, MSNBC, and Fox are all covering it."

"Did you hear anything about Escondido?" Frank asked.

"Yeah, dad, that was quite a deal."

"What did you hear?"

"The place got invaded by the enemy. The townspeople fought them, and won. That was the best advertisement for the NRA that I've ever seen."

"Interesting. You won't believe the kind of stories we've heard about that."

"More garbage from the nutcase internet sites?" Robbie asked. "You probably heard the pig blood story."

"Yes, and that the Army helped the enemy kill a bunch of citizens."

"Our Army?" Robbie asked.

"Yeah."

"That's a load of BS, dad. If somebody is telling you that, they're probably part of one of those militias. Some of them are trying to take advantage of the situation. If you're hearing that kind of crap from anybody, get away from them."

"Good advice. You take care, Robbie. We're gonna get going."

"Alright, dad, love you."

"Love you too, son. I'll give you back to mom."

Frank handed the phone back to Jane.

"Say goodbye. We're leaving. Now."

Jane gave him a funny look, and then put the phone to her ear.

"Goodbye, Robbie. I love you."

"Bye mom. Love you two." The phone clicked as Robbie hung up.

Frank fired up the engine and turned on the lights. He was slowly pulling out when he saw Dave running over with Hank.

"Where are you going, Frank?" shouted Dave.

"My daughter is in trouble. She's up in Oregon. We're heading that way now."

"That isn't advisable," Dave said. "You'll get blown off the road."

"I'll take my chances."

"We could make you stay," Hank said.

Frank pointed the pistol at him.

"Go ahead and try," Frank said. "We're out of here."

Suddenly Frank and Jane heard some of the other coaches start their engines. They started to line up, getting ready to follow. Hank and Dave backed away, and went running, trying to talk to the people in the first couple of coaches.

"Go go go!" said Jane. Frank got on the highway. Just as he was driving away, he heard a shotgun blast. He looked in his mirror and saw Hank stagger back and fall away from one of the coaches.

"Some of the folks in our party listened to their radios," Frank said.

"Probably," Jane said. "Or they called family members."

"I'm so lucky to be married to such a smart woman," Frank said, choking up. "I was ready to believe those creeps."

"I know," Jane said. "So was I. Wonder what they were planning to do?"

Frank started to cry. Jane looked over at him.

"What is it, Frank?"

"I killed a cop," Frank said, tears running down his cheeks.

“Frank, I wouldn’t worry about that too much. He was a bad guy. He was trying to hold us at that campground as the enemy was heading that way. Think about it.”

“Oh, crap,” Frank said, looking into his mirror. “Headlights to the left. Looks like that jeep. Grab the shotgun.”

Jane looked at Frank with horror, and then got out of her chair and picked up the shotgun from behind Frank’s seat. She pumped it once, chambering a shell.

The jeep pulled up alongside Frank. Dave was driving, and Ken was in the passenger seat, holding a rifle.

“Pull over now, Frank,” shouted Dave.

Chapter 10 - Let's Play Chicken

"Shoot his tire," Dave shouted.

Ken sat silently as the jeep and the RV careened down the road, speed increasing.

"C'mon, kid, take out his tire," shouted Dave.

"At this speed? Are you nuts?" Ken shouted back.

Frank looked over at them, listening to the argument, as he coaxed the big V-10 to go faster.

"Get back in your seat and belt yourself in, honey," he shouted to Jane. "Keep the shotgun on your lap."

Jane moved over and strapped into her seat.

"What are you planning to do?" Jane asked.

"See those lights coming at us in the other lane? Semi. Let's see if this idiot wants to play chicken with a 24,000 pound RV."

"Oh, Shit!" Jane said, looking down the road. "That truck is coming at us fast."

Frank looked in his rear-view mirror.

"Ha ha, the guy behind me knows what's up. He's pulling up close. Dave isn't going to have a place to get out of the way other than the ditch on the left side of the road."

“Boss, look,” cried Ken. Dave looked forward and his eyes got wide. He sped up. Frank did too.

“Can we outrun that jeep?” asked Jane.

“On a smooth flat surface, probably. I’m watching the tach. We still have some room, and we’re going almost 80.”

“Dave! Look out!” shouted Ken.

“I can’t outrun that V-10,” Dave shouted. He started slowing down. Then he saw that the coach behind Frank was pulled up nice and tight. He slowed down more. Same thing with the next coach.

“Boss, there’s nowhere to move right,” shouted Ken. The semi-truck was coming up fast, and it began to honk its horn.

“Put your hand out, and make that one move back,” Dave shouted.

Ken turned around in his seat and motioned to the coach to move back and let him in. The old man driving the coach flipped him off, and kept up his speed.

“They aren’t going to let us in, Boss. They’re on to us.”

“Hold on,” cried Dave. He turned the jeep off the road, hitting the soft shoulder. They were going too fast. The front wheels dug into the sand. The jeep cartwheeled into the desert floor, and rolled several times. The semi-truck flew by them, still honking its horn.

The coaches behind Frank and Jane honked their horns.

"Wow, I doubt either of them survived that," Jane said.

"Hopefully not," Frank said. He started slowing down, getting them to about 60.

"There was only two of those guys in the jeep. Wonder where the other one is?"

"Probably in that coach I see in the rear-view mirror. Its pulling off the road now, up to the crashed Jeep. Lewis wasn't in the jeep, so it's probably him."

"Hope he doesn't come after us," Jane said.

"I'll recognize the coach. It's a rare one. An old Winnebago Brave."

"Good. Wonder why Ken didn't shoot at us?"

"Don't know. And why the heck did they try to stop us anyway?"

"Probably because you spilled the beans about your internet knowledge," Jane said.

"More likely because they knew that most of us are packing, and they wanted the guns and supplies that we have. You saw that they tried to stop the other coaches from following us. I think they were going to herd us to their forces. We'll have to watch out that we don't fall victim to them later down the line."

Jane nodded.

The road ahead was clear. Every so often a car came the other way. It was usually a semi-truck. Lucy started to whine, looking up at Jane. She put the shotgun on the floor between the seats, and patted her lap.

"Come on up, girl," Jane said. Lucy jumped up. She was trembling again.

"That poor dog," Frank said, laughing. "This hasn't exactly been a relaxing vacation for her."

"So how far should we go tonight?"

"There are a lot of places to camp at the south rim of the Grand Canyon, and I suspect there are spaces available. Most of the European and Japanese tourists probably decided to wait until a more stable time to come over here."

"Good point, let's go there," Jane said. "Should we check with the others back there?"

"How?"

"Well, we could look for a good spot to pull over to the side of the road for a few minutes."

"Alright, Jane, why don't you see if you can find us a spot on your iPhone?"

"Will do." She picked up her phone and went to the map application.

"Sooner rather than later would be good," Frank said. "We're going up in elevation, and I see a lot more trees ahead. It'll probably be harder to find a nice big flat spot up there."

"I think I've found a place. There's a little road that is off to the right coming up, leading to a place called Sunset. There's a turnout right before the road. We should be able to park there. Looks pretty big."

"Alright, let me know when we're getting close."

"We're almost there now. Better start slowing down."

There was a sign that showed an intersection coming from the right. The lights of the coach shined on it brightly.

"There's the sign," Frank said. He started slowing down, and put on his right blinker.

"Look, they have asphalt along the side, and there's the road to Sunset," Jane said, pointing.

Frank turned over slowly, creeping along. He pulled up all the way to where the road to Sunset was, and then stopped. He shut off the engine, and looked in his mirror. All of the other coaches were parked.

"Let's leave the dog inside," Frank said. Jane nodded. They walked over to the door and opened it, hearing the steps go out under them. They stepped out, as several groups of people came walking over.

It took a few minutes for everybody to gather around.

"Wow, look at all the people," Jane said, standing next to Frank.

"Hi, everybody," Frank said in a loud voice. Several people said hi back, but most people nodded and looked at Frank, waiting to hear what he had to say.

"We're thinking of finding a place to camp on the south rim of the Grand Canyon, but we don't know this area very well. Anybody know of a better place to stop tonight?"

An older gentleman hobbled up. He had a cane.

"I've been around here a lot. Normally I'd say no way, because those campsites fill up this time of year. Half of Germany, Japan, and England are here." He started to laugh, but it turned into a wheeze. "I'll betcha most of those folks stayed home this year."

"That's what we were thinking," Jane said. "How's the drive from here? Is it OK in the dark? Is it close enough to make it before it gets too late?"

"Yes," said the old man. "It's not that far. I'm Chester, by the way."

"Hi, Chester. Frank and Jane here," said Frank. "Any campground suggestions?"

"The first one of the area is about as good as any. It's got lots of big pull through spaces, and 50 amp too."

"Agreed," another man said. "I was there last year. Nice place. Good people run it."

"Alright," Frank said. "Anybody object?"

Nobody said anything. Jane looked up at Frank, and then back out to the crowd.

"How did you find out about Dave?" she asked.

"I called my daughter and found out his stories were a lot of BS," one man said.

"Same here," said another person.

"Called family too," said another.

"One of those guys is still out there," Frank said. "Lewis. I think he's driving an old Winnebago Brave."

"Yep, that's him," Chester said. "He was the nicest of the bunch. I'd be surprised if he comes after us."

"Well, we'd better keep an eye out just in case," Frank said.

People nodded, and a few said yes.

"Alright, let's get going. See you guys there," Frank said. Everybody turned and walked back to their coaches. Frank got back into the driver's seat. Jane was about to climb into the passenger seat when she saw Mr. Wonderful sitting there.

"Hey, move it, big boy," Jane said. She pushed on him and he jumped off the seat. Frank laughed as he started the engine. They pulled back onto the road and got up to speed.

"We need to be careful, if we don't want to end up leading this expedition," Jane said.

"I know. They're looking for somebody to lead them. They all thought that was Dave before. Wonder how many of them knew him before this mess started?"

"Good question."

The scenery was getting more and more beautiful as they went along, even at night. There were signs advertising various campgrounds, resorts, and tour companies.

"Looks like we aren't that far," Frank said.

"According to my GPS, we're still at least an hour away."

"How's your battery holding up?"

"We have enough to get there, I think," Jane said. "I could plug it into the socket behind the seat, I suppose."

"Might be a good idea."

"Alright," Jane said. She got up and went into the bedroom to get the charger. She plugged it in behind her seat and set it down on the floor. “No eating my cellphone, Miss Lucy.” The dog perked up, and wanted to climb back up on Jane’s lap. She jumped up as Jane was sitting down.

“What do you think our longer-term plan ought to be?” Frank asked.

“I don’t know. I was thinking about that, though. I wish we could go home, but we’ll need to wait and watch. At least we know we can get news and use the phones.”

“Well, we think we can at this point, at least,” Frank said

“You aren’t still believing in these anti-government stories, are you?”

“No, but I’m worried about all of these militias. We may run into them out on the roads. They may be a danger.”

“Oh. Yeah, you could be right about that,” Jane said.

“I’m not a hundred percent sure about the government, either, to be honest. This border thing is lousy management at best. You have to agree with me there. We should never have allowed things to get to this point.”

Jane sighed, and nodded yes.

They were silent for a little while, as the miles rolled by. Then they saw a big string of headlights coming at them from the north.

“Lots of folks coming,” Frank said.

“Looks like another military convoy.”

It was upon them in minutes. They drove past the line of RVs as if they weren’t there.

“Wow, there must be about 30 troop transport trucks in this line up.”

“Here come some tanks,” Jane said, pointing.

“More battle tanks. And this time I know why they need them. We’ll be taking southern Arizona back in short order, I suspect.”

“Well, so much for the Federal troops being a danger to us,” Jane said, shaking her head.

“Hopefully they run into Dave’s buddies.”

“If he has any left,” Jane said. “If it’s just Lewis, he’s probably already disappeared into the woodwork.”

“He knows I shot Officer Simmons.”

“Remember, though, that he didn’t see it. Dave and Ken were the only ones who saw that, and I doubt if either of them walked away from that crash.”

“You’re probably right about that, but I can’t help worrying about this. I wonder if I should contact the authorities and tell them what happened?”

“Don’t do that, Frank,” Jane said. “I wouldn’t worry about it. If he was still in that ditch, he probably got burned up in the fire fight that happened there. Remember the napalm?"

"True. I still wish I wouldn't have had to do that. It's not a good feeling. I'll never get over it. I keep seeing his face."

"That's because you're a good man, Frank."

They passed Tusayan, a small town at the gateway of the Grand Canyon National Park.

"We're getting close now," Jane said. "I'd better get my phone back up here."

She got up and pulled the phone charger out of the wall socket, then got back in her seat with it in her hand.

"Close?" asked Frank.

"Yes, we're only about ten miles away," she said.

"Good, hopefully we can relax at this place for a little while. A day or two at least."

"That would be wonderful."

They drove along, and started to see more cars coming and going on the side streets. There were roads going off to National Park campgrounds.

"You don't think Chester was talking about one of those?" asked Jane.

"No, I think he was talking about a place with hookups. Do you want to boondock? I don't."

"No boondocking for me tonight, if we can avoid it."

"Wonder if that's it?" asked Frank, pointing to a driveway with an RV Park sign, coming up dead ahead.

Just then a coach behind him beeped their horn twice.

"Yeah, this is it," Jane said. "Turn in."

Frank nodded and pulled into the long driveway. A man came out of the office. He had a shotgun in his hands.

"Uh oh," Jane said.

"Be calm. I'd do that too, given the circumstances."

The man came around to their driver's side window. Frank opened it. The man looked like an old cowboy.

"Where you folks coming from?" He sounded like an old cowboy, too.

"We're from Southern California, but we came up through southern Arizona. We're looking for a safe place."

"You aren't some of those militia nuts, are you?"

"No, we just got away from some of those folks."

"Hey, Charlie!" shouted Chester from the coach behind them. The man looked back, squinting. Then he looked at Frank.

"You guys with Chester?"

"Yes, he's one of our group. There are about 20 of us."

Charlie got a great big grin on his face.

"Go on in. We have plenty of open spaces. Just come back to the office after you pick one. I need the space number." He smiled and waved them forward.

"Whew," Jane said.

Frank looked in his rear-view mirror, and saw Charlie and Chester. They hugged, patting each other's backs.

"Yep, Chester and Charlie are close, it looks like," Frank said. "I just saw them hug back there."

"Good. Maybe we'll get some rest this time."

"Seriously."

They drove down the center street. There were rows of slanted pull through spaces on either side, with plenty of shade trees. Up ahead of them were about twenty park models. They appeared to be occupied, as light was shining out the windows and from the porch lights.

"Let's go down this row," Frank said, and he turned in. He went down to the end and pulled into the space. It was deep enough to fit both the RV and the toad.

"This looks very nice," Jane said. Frank shut off the engine and got out of his seat. He stretched. Lucy jumped off Jane's lap, her tail wagging.

"I'd better take her out," Jane said. She got up, and put the leash on Lucy's collar.

Frank went to the door and opened it. He could see coaches pulling up, in the spaces to the right of them on their row, and also in the rows behind them and in front of them. There was the sound of people greeting each other and laughing. He stepped out, and was followed by Jane and Lucy.

"Wow, look at everyone!" Jane said. Lucy was attempting to pull her all over the place. "Slow down, girl."

"Yeah, we've got quite a crowd here. I'll bet the park owners are glad to see us. They should be full of tourists this time of year."

Chester came walking up. Frank walked out to greet him, and shook his hand.

"Thanks so much for telling us about this place, Chester. Now I feel like we can rest for a little while."

"You're quite welcome. Charlie and I go way back. He said to invite everybody to the clubhouse in a half hour. He's got a bunch of ice cream that he needs to get out of his freezer. I'm making the rounds telling everyone."

"Sounds great!" Frank said. Chester gave Frank a mock salute and continued on to the next coach.

"You really want to go?" Jane asked. "Aren't you tired?"

"Yes, I'm tired, but we should go there and see who we're with," Frank said. "We helped each other out on that road. We're stronger if we're together."

"Alright, you have a point. Let's get the coach put together."

They got done with the setup quickly.

"Hey, honey, could you check around for Mr. Wonderful? I want to put the slides out."

"Sure." She looked around, and found him in the back under the end of the bed. "He's in a good space, go ahead and do it."

"Thanks," Frank said. He got the slides out quickly

"I love the way Mr. Wonderful comes to attention and looks around when the slide starts moving out with him on it." She laughed.

"Yeah. I'm surprised he doesn't just bolt. Every other cat I've ever had would have done that."

“Mr. Wonderful isn’t every other cat,” she said.

“Okay, that’s it. We're all set up. You can turn off the water pump. I’ve got us connected to city water already.”

“Alright,” Jane said, switching it off as she came out into the front of the coach.

“I think we can just leave the Jeep connected,” Frank said. “If it makes sense to stick around here for a few days, we can unhook her in the morning.”

“Sounds good. I’ll just freshen up a little, and then we can walk over to the clubhouse. I see a lot of people heading in that direction out the window.”

“I guess I could run a comb through my hair, too.”

They were done with their grooming in a couple of minutes, and left the coach. Lucy wanted to go, but Frank pushed her back, shut the door, and locked up. There were still people walking in the direction of the clubhouse, which was bleeding light all over the front end of the park.

“This is a nice place,” Jane said. “I hope we can rest for a few days here.”

“Me too,” Frank said. He was really tired. “I’m glad this isn’t a very long walk.”

Frank and Jane followed another couple into the double doors of the clubhouse, which were held open with doorstops on both sides. The room had a stage at the far end, and rows of long tables in the middle. Off to the left side was a long table, with several commercial sized containers of ice cream. There were two young women behind them, dishing out ice cream into plastic bowls and handing them to people who were lined up. When some of people saw Jane and Frank standing inside the door way, they started clapping.

"Oh, my," Jane said, embarrassed. The applause continued for about thirty seconds.

Frank held up his hands.

"Thanks, folks, but we didn't do anything. We're just folks like the rest of you."

"You could have chickened out a couple of times," said one man. "If it wasn't for you, who knows where those creeps would have led us."

"Nice game of chicken!" shouted another man. The crowd burst into laughter.

"Yeah, well several of you helped out a lot with that," Frank said. "Nice job of slamming the door on those guys."

Chester hobbled over slowly, with Charlie following him. They had wide grins on their faces.

"Get some ice cream, folks, before it melts too much," Charlie said. "Then we'll talk."

Frank nodded, and he and Jane walked over to the table. They got bowls of ice cream from one of the pretty young ladies that was dishing it out. She had a sweet smile.

"Here you go," she said.

They walked back over to the table where Charlie and Chester were sitting.

"It's so nice of you to feed us ice cream," Jane said. Then she took a spoonful. "Oh, this is heavenly."

"My pleasure," Charlie said. "It helps me out too. I need the freezer space. I shot a couple deer yesterday, and need to put a bunch of that meat in there."

"Food delivery is becoming a problem, I suspect," Frank said.

"Yes, at least fresh stuff like meat and certain vegetables. I've got a lot of canned food and a lot of frozen food, and a lot of dry goods. Having fresh meat right now really helps."

"If you don't mind poaching, that is," Chester said, laughing.

"Well, true, Chester, I'm poaching. We have too many deer around here anyway, and the authorities have bigger fish to fry at this point."

"How has it been around here?" asked Jane.

"Bad," Charlie said. "All of the foreign business is gone at this point. We just have stragglers like yourselves coming in, on the way to somewhere else."

"Any violence happening here?" Frank asked.

"Not at my place, but we've been able to scare away trouble makers, and this place isn't out of the way far enough for the militias to be interested. We still have a functioning town, and people still live here."

"There's been problems at other RV parks?"

"Not so much at RV parks, but at campgrounds. The worst are the boondocking places like the National Park campsites," Charlie said. "These nuts want to be off the grid, for the most part, so they hang out over there. The only thing that worries me is that they might decide to make some supply raids."

"They're probably well-armed," Frank said.

"Yeah, but so are we, and they're stupid," Charlie said.

"Yup, like that idiot Dave and his buddies," Chester said.

"How did you guys hook up with him, anyway?" Jane asked.

"I didn't exactly hook up with him. I lived in Williams," Chester said. "Dave and Ken and Lewis were deputies, but they weren't what I would call bright. They were preppers, and bought into all of this secession nonsense. It was okay to have them in the department when the Chief was still functioning, but at the end he could barely cope with the job and his wife's Alzheimer's. When things started to go sideways, he was done. It's a shame. He was a good man. I grew up with him. And his wife was a gem."

"Did you follow Dave and his friends out into that campsite?" asked Jane.

"No," Chester said. "We didn't really want anything to do with them. We'd been camped out there for a couple weeks when they showed up. They convinced most of us to turn off our cell phones."

"We got the same story from them, but we already had ours off after an earlier experience, with some couple that was in Yuma."

"Yuma, huh," Charlie said. "Heard about problems down there."

"I'll tell you all about it tomorrow," Frank said. "But I think we ought to get some sleep. I'm exhausted."

"Me too," Jane said. "Is it safe to stay here for a few days?"

"Depends on how the battle goes," Charlie said. "The enemy has taken over Tucson and the southern suburbs of Phoenix. If our army can't stop them from taking Phoenix, it will be time to get the heck out of here."

"That sounds scary," Chester said.

"Yes, old friend, it's scary," Charlie said. "If they take Phoenix, Flagstaff will be next."

"Any news from California or New Mexico?" Frank asked.

"Southern New Mexico is gone, but the enemy got stopped at the Texas border, and now the Texans are taking that state back piece by piece. California is the interesting one. It's not like these southwest states. It's wall to wall citizens in that state, and there is a shocking number of guns in civilian hands. Townspeople there have been winning battles in places that the army can't get to fast enough. The enemy got stopped in the middle of San Diego County. And then there is the naval base and Camp Pendleton right there. Southern California is being used as a staging area from which to pound the enemy as they are coming up through Mexico."

"Maybe we should go back there," Jane said.

"You won't be able to get back in, at least for a little while," Charlie said. "They don't want the enemy flanking them from Arizona or Nevada, so they have the California border sealed up tight."

"Alright," Frank said. "We'll chat more tomorrow. Let's go, honey."

The couple stood up, shook hands with Chester and Charlie, and headed for the door. They walked back to their coach through the cool night air. Other people were heading back too.

Lucy heard them walking up to the door of the rig, and started barking.

"Why don't you take her out, Frank, while I get the rig ready for bedtime?"

"No problem," Frank said. He unlocked the door and opened it. Lucy came bounding out. Frank reached inside the door for the leash, hooked her up, and took her out.

Jane got the blinds closed down, put dry food and water out for the pets, and turned down the bed. She was just getting into her nightgown when Frank came back in with Lucy.

“Mission accomplished,” he said. “Wow, I should have come back sooner.” He watched Jane’s naked silhouette as she pulled her nightgown in place.

“Down, boy,” Jane said. “You’re tired, remember?”

“Not that tired,” he replied, walking back into the bedroom.

Frank turned out the lights, and closed the bedroom door. He got ready for bed, and then got in and moved close to Jane’s soft warm form.

“Are we going to be alright, Frank?”

“I think so, sweetheart,” he said. Then he moved over and kissed her. They caressed and hugged, becoming more and more urgent. They pulled their night clothes off each other frantically and forgot about the world for a while.

Chapter 11 - After A Night of Peace

Frank woke up to the alarm on his cellphone. It was 6:00. He stretched. Mr. Wonderful heard the alarm, because he bumped the bedroom door, and started his usual feeding time meows, which were constant until food was delivered.

"Alright, alright, Mr. Wonderful," he said, stretching again. Jane stirred, but didn't wake up. He got up, threw on some short pants and a shirt, and slid open the door, trying to be quiet enough to let Jane sleep a little longer. Mr. Wonderful rubbed against his leg, and continued to meow. Lucy looked in Frank's direction, but stayed on her perch, on the back of the couch.

Frank walked over to the fridge, opened the door, pulled out the cat and dog food cans, and dished it up. The dog and cat scampered over and started eating as soon as he set their dishes down.

"Coffee," Frank said to himself. He turned on the coffee maker and waited for it to heat up. Soon the coach was filled with the smell of coffee brewing, and Frank was having his first cup.

"Wonder if there's Wi-Fi here?" he asked himself. He grabbed his laptop from the closet, and set it up on the dinette table. Lucy came running over, tail wagging, trying to get his attention.

"OK, girl, I know you need to go out." Frank got up, and got Lucy's leash attached. He followed her down the steps with coffee cup in hand. She was in a hurry to get to the patch of grass next to the concrete slab they were parked on. The morning was crisp and clear. Frank looked around. The park was peaceful. Most people were still asleep. Lucy led him around their space, and over to the flag road. He walked her down that, looking at the coaches. Most were newer models, 2015 and up. About half were diesel units, and they were considerably bigger than his 34-foot rig. Some people looked like they were ready for a long stay. One place had their patio furniture under the awning already, plus a string of globe lights hanging down, and a couple of pink flamingos stuck in the grass next to them.

There was a man sitting under his awning having a cup of coffee in the last space before the main access road. He rose as he saw Frank coming, and walked out to greet him. He looked like a mountain man – a scrawny form in jeans, a flannel shirt, and boots. He had a big grey beard.

"You're Frank, right?" he asked, extending his hand.

"Yes," Frank replied, shaking hands.

"I'm Jeb. Good to meet you."

"Where are you from, Jeb?"

"New Mexico," he said. "I got out of there just in time. I grew up around here, though. Where are you from?"

"Redondo Beach, California. We got out with time to spare. I actually wish I would have stuck around there now. We would have probably been okay, and the authorities have things locked down pretty well now, according to my son."

"Still there, is he? I think you are gonna be glad you're not there. Martial Law gets old really fast."

"Well, you have a point there, I would imagine."

"Hey, I look at this like snow birding," Jeb said. "Right now things are nicer away from the areas that have Martial Law. Kinda like snow. I'll wait till the thaw to go back."

Frank laughed.

"Funny you should put it that way. I used a similar argument to talk my wife into leaving."

"Great minds think alike, I guess." Both men laughed.

"Well, from what I hear, I can't get back into SoCal anyway. It's bottled up to keep the enemy from crossing in and flanking the Feds."

"Even if they were letting people in, could you imagine how many checkpoints you'd have to go through? And most of them would want to search your rig."

"True enough," Frank replied. "Well, I'd better get back. Time for a refill."

"Alright, Frank. Nice talkin with you."

Frank coaxed Lucy back in the direction of their coach. People were starting to get up, and several waved at him or said good morning as he walked by. He opened the coach door, and Lucy bounded in. Frank sat down in front of his laptop and moved the mouse to get the screensaver off. Then he went to the network settings and looked for Wi-Fi. He had a strong signal, so he clicked on the connect button. There was a password required.

"Shoot," he said. Jane came walking out of the bedroom. Her hair was disheveled, and she was pulling her nightgown back on.

Frank got a devilish grin on his face.

"Well, don't you look well..."

"Shut up, Frank," she said with an embarrassed grin. "I hope the neighbors didn't hear us."

Frank laughed. "I don't care if they did."

Jane shook her head, smiling. She pulled a coffee cup out of the cupboard and put it on the coffee maker, and then put a pod into the machine and pressed brew.

"Ahhhhh, that smells so good," she said. The machine finished with a sputter, and she picked up her cup and had a sip.

"I'm going to have to go to the office. The Wi-Fi is asking for a password."

"Alright. You go ahead, Frank. I'm not ready to go outside yet."

"No problem. I have to give Charlie our space number and pay up, anyway."

"What space are we in? I didn't see it posted."

"We're in 216. It's hard to see in the dark, but I saw it this morning when I was walking Lucy."

"You might want to put out the awning on your way out. We're going to have some heat today."

"I know, it's already getting warm outside. Turn on the AC when you need to."

"Okay," Jane said. "Probably better to do that before it gets too warm in here."

Frank got up and went for the door. Lucy jumped up, tail wagging. He pushed the button to extend the awning, and watched it moving out through the window.

"Sorry, girl, you have to stay here this time. Daddy's got business to do."

Jane laughed.

"Better put on your hat, or you'll burn," she said.

Frank nodded, and grabbed his baseball cap on the way out. He walked down to the end of the flag road, waving at Jeb as he went by, and then turned right on the main road and walked over to the office. A bell rang when he opened the door.

Charlie was sitting at a desk, looking at a computer screen when Frank came in. He looked up and smiled at Frank, and then walked up to the counter.

"We're in space 216," Frank said. "How much do we owe you?"

"It's $25 a night. Is that okay?" Charlie asked.

"Sure, sounds good. You take plastic?"

"Yes, that's still working. How many nights do you plan on staying?"

"Good question," Frank said. "Why don't I pay you for three, and we'll go from there?"

He passed his card across the counter to Charlie.

"Alright. If things go bad down south, I'll let all of you know. In fact, I'll be clearing out of here too if that happens."

"Okay. How about the Wi-Fi?"

"The password is *southrimRV*. Not too hard to figure out."

"Any restrictions?"

"Normally I ask that people don't stream movies, but the system was built for 400 coaches. We've only got about 40 here now, so don't worry about it."

"Great, thanks," Frank said.

"What do you folks plan to do?"

"We just want to hang out somewhere safe until we can get back into SoCal."

"How about the rest of the group?"

"I have no idea," Frank said. "We just met yesterday. Nice group of people, from what I can tell so far."

"I think they're looking at you as a leader."

"I got that impression, but I wasn't planning on taking that on," Frank said. "I just happened to be in the front of the line yesterday when we left the Williams area."

"Well, from what I've heard from Chester, they could do a lot worse."

Frank just smiled.

"You and Chester go back quite a ways, I take it."

"Yes, he's been a friend for years. We grew up together, although he was a little older than the rest of us. He's up here a few times a year."

"Nice place, by the way. I'm sure we'll be back during happier times."

"I hope so, Frank. This park has been in the family for a long time. My grandpa started it in the twenties, and my dad took it over later. Now it's mine."

"Well, I guess I'll get back. Nice talking to you."

"Yeah, same here."

Frank walked out the door and headed back to his coach. Lots of people were up and around now, giving him more waves and 'Good Mornings' as he walked down the road.

He got back to his coach just as Jane was raising the blinds at the windshield. He waved to her, walked to the door, and opened it.

"Why don't you pull out the chairs and table before you come in?"

"Good idea," Frank said. He went back to the rear storage compartment, opened it, and took out four chairs and the table. He was setting them up when Jane walked out the door with Lucy on her leash.

"Nice out here," Jane said. She was dressed in short shorts and a sleeveless button down top.

"Sure is. I bought us three more nights. It's not too expensive - $25 per night. Oh, and I got the password for the Wi-Fi also."

"You think it's safe for us to stay here that long?"

"Probably, but if things go south down in Phoenix, we'll take off. Charlie is watching the situation, and he'll take off too if they start making their way to Flagstaff."

"You going to unhook the Jeep?"

"Only if you want to go somewhere," Frank said.

"Alright, then let's play that by ear. We're still in good shape for supplies."

Frank nodded, and then went into the coach.

"Going to get on the internet?" Jane asked.

He poked his head back out the door. "Yes, I want to check out what's going on."

"Alright, but don't stay on too long. I want you to go to the pool with me in a little while."

Frank nodded yes, and went into the coach. He sat down in front of his laptop and went back to the login page. The password got him onto the network in seconds, and he opened his email. There was a message from Sarah asking how he and her mother were doing, and saying that things were good up in Oregon. There was an email from the storage yard, saying that they had weathered the bad times and were fully in business. The rest of the messages were just advertisements and tickler messages from news and political websites he had joined. He typed a quick reply to Sarah telling her where they were and what was going on, and copied Robbie. Then he went to the news pages. He spent the next hour looking at every one of his usual sources, soaking up the situation in the southwest, Mexico, Iraq, Venezuela, and other places. Jane came in looking for him at that point.

"Can we go to the pool now?" Jane asked.

"Sure, sorry," he said. He followed Jane into the bedroom, and they changed into their swimsuits. When Jane had her suit on, Frank came up behind her and put his arms around her waist. She tensed up for a second, then relaxed.

"Down, boy," Jane said, looking at him with a smile.

"Oh, alright," Frank said. He kissed her on the forehead.

They picked up their towels and walked towards the door.

"Honey, let's leave the air conditioner on for Lucy, alright?"

"Of course, I was planning on it," Frank said. Lucy was right at the door, wagging her tail.

"Sorry, girl, you'll have to wait inside for a little while," Jane said. They left the coach and Frank locked it up.

"Hope she doesn't mind too much," Frank said as they walked away.

"She'll be fine. Tell me what you saw on the internet."

"Well, good news, bad news, and scary news," Frank said.

"Does it look like we're safe here?"

"Maybe. The problem is that most of our troops are busy in Texas and along the California/Mexico border. They're slowly moving assets here, but the enemy is controlling I-10 and has blown up some sections of I-40. They're trying to move men and tanks from California via I-15 and Route 89, and also from the east down Routes 160 and 89, but it's slow going."

"Is that the bad news or the scary news?"

"That's the bad news. The scary news is that forces coming from Texas are pushing the enemy out of New Mexico, and they're on their way here. Even if we hold Phoenix, the area we are in now might become a problem in the next few days. To make matters worse, most of the folks coming this way are the Islamist fighters, and they've been pretty hard on the civilian populations. Sounds like they're doing what Hank was talking about. Without the Feds helping them, of course."

"So we might not be able to relax here for a while."

"Probably not, but it depends. We might be getting air transport on line here in the next couple of days. They were all being used in SoCal before. C-17s and other heavy transport planes. If that happens we'll have a flood of military folks coming in to take on the Islamists."

"So what's the good news?"

"We've pushed the enemy all the way out of California now, and are using resources there to really pound all of the routes to the south that the enemy was using to enter the US, both through California and Arizona. That's where most of the air power is being used right now."

"How come they aren't using air power here?"

“Well, they are using some, but they aren’t going to come in and carpet bomb Tucson or Phoenix. We’d lose too many American civilians. Washington is being very careful about this.”

“Makes sense, I guess,” Jane said. “What about the civilians in Southern Arizona and in New Mexico? They aren’t doing as well against the enemy as we saw in SoCal?”

“Not really. Remember what we were talking about last night. The population density is too low. It was a lot easier for the enemy to surround the major population centers, when they don’t have millions and millions of folks with guns pointed at them. It’s not like people aren’t fighting back. They are, but they haven’t been in a position to destroy the enemy like we did in SoCal.”

“Alright. So we may not get to stay here,” Jane said. She had a disappointed look on her face. They got to the pool, and walked through the gate. There were a few other people there, but plenty of open lounge chairs that they could put their stuff on. They set down their towels and cell phones and walked over to the shallow end.

“A little cold,” Frank said, sticking his foot in.

"Don't be as sissy," Jane said. She quickly got in up to her neck, and then dunked her head under the water. Frank followed her in and did the same.

"Ahh, this feels great," Jane said. Frank nodded, wiping his eyes.

"So what other news did you see?"

Frank dunked his head one more time, and shook his head to get some of the water to run out of his hair.

"Political stuff. There's a big fight going on in Washington about martial law. The Administration wants to declare it over the lower 48 states. They're saying that it makes it easier to route military and supplies into the battle zones when they have control of the roads and can close them to trucks and other traffic quickly."

"And I imagine that the House and Senate are fighting that tooth and nail," Jane said. "Same old same old."

"Yeah, except the ACLU and several other organizations that are usually liberal are on the same side with the conservatives and libertarians on this one. Reminds me of the NSA scandal a couple of years ago."

"So what do you think, Frank, after we've been out here for a while?"

"About martial law everywhere? Think about it. We might not have gotten out of harm's way yesterday if they had the roads bottled up."

"True, but we might not have had crazy ex-police officers trying to stop us either."

"Or those same crazy folks would have been able to stop us easier, because they might still have been in charge. Remember Officer Simmons."

"Alright, you have a point. Maybe we should be continuing north today instead of hanging out here, just in case they slam the door shut."

"I was thinking the same thing. We could take Route 89, and maybe get all the way up to Capitol Reef by early evening. Then the next day we could get on I-15 and travel to the other side of Salt Lake City. Maybe that would be far enough away for a while."

"What if the battle goes well in Phoenix, and we can use those forces to stop the enemy from coming over from New Mexico?"

"We can wait and see, but if things go south we may have to haul ass out of here. I don't want to be around if those helicopters come this way."

"Wonder how much warning we'd get?"

"Good question," Frank said. "But I'm also worried about the martial law thing. The Administration is saying that they have the power to put that into effect without the Congress going along with it. I wouldn't put that past them. We might get stuck too close to the battle zone if it happens."

"Do you think all of the local law enforcement folks would go along with that?"

"That's another good question, my dear." Frank moved closer to Jane and put his arms around her waist, pulling her against him.

"I guess I really got to you last night," she said, with an embarrassed smile.

"Well, yes. It could just be the excitement of being on the run."

"You may have a point there, sweetie. Maybe that had a lot to do with my performance last night."

Frank backed away from her, acting offended.

"What, it wasn't my prowess?

Jane splashed him, laughing. Frank splashed her back, and soon they were giggling like teenagers, in a full-on water fight.

"Frank," somebody said from the side of the pool. Frank and Jane looked up. It was

Charlie, standing next to a police officer and an Army officer.

"What's up?" Frank asked.

"These two gentlemen want to talk to you about Williams."

To Be Continued in Bug Out! Book 2 – available now!

Copyright

About the Author

Robert G Boren is a writer from the South Bay section of Southern California. He writes Short Stories, Novels, and Serialized Fiction. Most of his work is centered in and around South Bay, or is about South Bay people.

Other Books by Robert Boren

Bug Out! Texas is now for sale in the Kindle Store.

America is under attack! "Bug Out! Texas" is the story of Texas Patriots who fight the invaders

In the ***Bug Out!*** Series, Foreign Terrorists, Secessionist Militias, and a corrupt Federal Government make war on the American People.

Bug Out! Texas covers the war behind the sealed borders of Texas.

Texas has become a major gateway for terrorists crossing the border.

How will the invasion play out in a state with freedom-loving people and a minimum of gun control laws?

Regular folks from all walks of life join the fight as corrupt political operatives try to stop them.

Bug Out! Texas is full of action and romance, as people rely on each other to survive and fight.

Bug Out! Texas is a sweeping story. Citizens go mobile in their *RVs* to escape and to attack, rushing from one part of the huge state to another.

There's action in the cities, in the woods, on the plains, and on Falcon Lake. Will the people prevail?

Find out in Bug Out! Texas Book 1.

Horror Road - A Supernatural Thriller

Horror Road Book 1 - A Supernatural Thriller is a story of ancient spirits, ghosts, psychics, and killers.

Written by the author of Bug Out!, this series starts where the *Bug Out!* series left off, at an isolated RV Park in Kansas.

There is an evil presence at the RV Park. It has awakened due to the presence of powerful *psychics* Jake and Frankie, and now it threatens them with *possession*.

Related *paranormal* activity begins at two other locations, resulting in gruesome deaths.

Jake and Frankie can see what is happening as the evil presence reveals itself to them. Can they stop it?

Ghosts become more active as the spirit's plans take shape.

Jake and Frankie know that they must join forces with another group of psychics to battle the *pure evil* which is tormenting them, but they are over a thousand miles away.

A powerful **medium** has awakened, ready to do battle, but so have new minions of the ancient evil. It's a race against time and space.

Pick up this tale of Supernatural Horror today!

Never A Loose End - The Franklin and Davis Files Book One

Serial Killers. Maniac Ex-cops. CIA Assassins. White Slavers. Strippers

In *"Never A Loose End"*, they all come together, racing towards their frightening destiny.

This is the story that started it all for George Franklin and Malcolm Davis. Some of you know them from the later episodes of the *Bug Out!* series, set seven years later. This is the story of how they met, and the battle that forged them into a formidable team.

George and Malcolm are both targets, marked for death, but why?

A clan of Serial Killers is active again, after hiding for years. What has brought them out?

Follow George and Malcolm as they dash through the Southwest in
their ***Motorhomes.***

Murder, gun battles, bombings, and general mayhem reign in "Never A Loose End"

Who will survive? Will the hunted be brought down, or will they become the *hunters* instead?

Find out in "Never A Loose End - The Franklin and Davis Files Book One"

Note: This full-length novel carries a hard R rating, unlike the PG-13 Bug Out! series. "Never A Loose End" contains graphic violence and sex. Discretion is advised.

Made in the USA
Lexington, KY
22 July 2018